I'd love to kill, please

A Novel

Dan Jones

Cover design by Samantha Smeaton

Cover illustrations by Dan Jones

ISBN 9798287138653

Dedicated to a few ...

AUNT BARBARA

My second proofreader who powered through the filthy

segments.

Your selfless force endures.

STRANGER/MUSE

A seventy-four-year-old man with a cane, puppy, and

history.

Nice to meet you.

PAPA

The antithesis of Lance.

A caring grandfather to my children.

An inspiration for unwavering, concise kindness.

CHAPTER 1

It is maddening.

It is not all I have.

It is not an "it."

It is murder.

I haven't done it. I don't know that I want to. I don't know that I don't want to.

I'm a single-minded guy. An only child. No kids. Probably a shut-in. Strong-but-silent type. Used to play football. Couldn't keep the girls off me. Was good looking. Still am. I look good for my age. I'm told that. If someone doesn't say it first, I will.

I was also an ass. Still am. My wife says so.

I never married until five years ago. I enjoy her company, she enjoys mine. She tells me I'm a dick, an asshole, insensitive, arrogant, and too quiet, contradictions I don't feel like getting into during this walk. I respect how she puts me in my place.

There's that man again. He looks like me. If there's a way to time travel, that's me running. Fuck, look at him go. Look at his body. I sound like a fag, but I don't give a shit. If I were a woman, I'd fuck that guy. If I were a lesbian, I'd want to fuck him. And I guess the gay guy would want to fuck him, too. I'm not gay, so I can't say anything about that. But I can see a gay guy wanting to suck his dick, at least. His body is so goddamned tone for a white guy. Jesus-Christ-Bruce-Lee-Brad-Pitt lean. Is he balding? Thinning? I think so. He must be older than I thought. Or he's unfortunate. One of those balding in his early twenties. But, no, he'd start that shit by eighteen or twenty if he's in his mid-to-late twenties. There'd be more hair missing. So, he's thinning. Which means he's older than late twenties.

Speculations get me in trouble. They always have. Assuming has ruined decades of my life. All those parts rubbed out because of not thinking right.

I'm going to make a guess and say he's thirty-three. Like Jesus. (Wasn't Bruce Lee around that age when he died? When did Brad Pitt get famous for his bod? Same age?) This man's jogging to his death, right to the cross. Maybe I'm the one who's going to catch him and put him up there. Drive stakes through his hands or wrists. Maybe put one between his eyes, through his forehead. No torture. I don't want to torture anyone. I don't have a need to inflict pain. I've done a lot of that. I've had so many fucking fights, I can't remember the first one.

That's a lie. I haven't been in many fights or brawls. It's just a go-to phrase. Isn't it?

I remember hitting my dad. He told me to have at it. He wasn't drunk. He wasn't slapping my mom around. He wasn't trying to hurt me or my sister (having no sister, using a general example from other families of retaliation). He wanted me to be tough inside of a specific moment. I wasn't crying. He wasn't being a man's man. Or maybe he was. I think he was proving to himself he was man enough to make me a man at three or whatever age I was when he said, "Try kicking me in the family jewels." That's what I remember. Traumatic? I guess. I didn't understand. Sure, I knew hitting didn't feel good and was something that came out of anger or self-protection. But I wasn't mad at my dad. I wasn't afraid. I also wasn't a bad kid. Not when I was three.

"I just want you to try," he said. "It's okay. Just tryyyyy." Maybe that's my memory slowing down that bit, putting an echo on the word like a crappy movie editor. Or maybe that's the heat making me sluggish, slowing my head, causing my body to reach out to the wall here.

I think I almost passed out just now. It's not the dad thought's doing. I think about that moment all the time. Not all the time, but I remember it. I've told the story. I've probably changed the incident from 50% fiction/50% fact to 90%/10%, fiction entertaining me in so many ways.

Maybe what's making me feel awful is Brad Pitt and Bruce Lee fighting folks in movies, and maybe I'm wondering how much they fought in real life, and maybe I'm thinking of how much I've been fighting back (getting confused, too, since Brad Pitt recently fought Bruce Lee in a movie).

At my age, slipping unconscious alterations into my memories and thoughts (since a thought becomes a memory right after you have it) is one of the best forms of entertainment I've got in this world.

Betty, the wife, is another good thing I've got. She's a button. Cute. Manageable. Five years younger than me. Smart enough and just right in the dumb aisle. *Like him*, I'm sure people think. I don't give a shit. I never have. People are going to like you, love you, hate you, or leave you. And if they leave you, you weren't anything to them.

I'm something and sure of it. Someone to remember. Someone people have had to hold down. I've been arrested. I've had surgeries. I've gone by fake names. I've falsified my image when using my real name. I even played blind for two whole days (but not once I'd left the city and drove home or ate dinner or whatever else the evenings brought).

I like who I am. That's how I'm feeling right now. I've

hated myself. I've wished things. I've gotten some of those wishes without asking for them to be granted.

Watching that man jog and sweat (in a non-homosexual way), I'm feeling good about my life. Ready to do a hell of a lot more.

CHAPTER 2

"Well, Butt, I don't know what to tell you," I say to Betty.

"I wish I would have known."

"I told you."

"You didn't."

"Okay. But I did."

"Nope."

"I fuckin' told ya!" I holler, because that's how I release my inner exaggeration, which isn't exactly the same as frustration. Betty Butt and I have discussed this.

"Shush yourself," she says. "And don't drink."

"I'm drinking as soon as we get there, because I won't be able to stand it otherwise."

"Why then, tell me, are we going?"

"Isn't it an award celebration for Bruce?" I ask, uncertain. She doesn't answer. "He supported me with my retirement." She's not saying anything. I groan as I struggle with my socks. "Another before-you-die party, right?" Nothing. Does she know I'm vulnerable? Do I? I must. "And I'm not going to not go. I'm going to go. I'm going to get drunk. And I goddamn told you and you forgot." I stand, socks and shoes on. "And you're making us late, so, I'll have to catch up on the drinking."

"You're not going to get shitfaced," Bettys says, coming out of the bathroom dressed and perfumed.

"Yes, I am, Butt."

"Lance, I hate you."

I kiss her like a movie to make this moment nice. A

peck that should break the tension and remind her this argument isn't worth it. Our love is better. But she turns away, giving me her ass side. One of the reasons I call her Butt.

Betty's full name is Elizabeth. Not hard to remember, although I've taken longer than five seconds to give up the wife's birth title when asked for it. A blank stare. Looking like a liar or a piece of shit. I swear to Christ, you'd think I'd kidnapped her. I've been told the whole of my face—the expression and whatever character I have behind this skin and stubbles of gray—vanishes. "Elizabeth" escapes me, her life and mine immediately drained from acknowledgment, and I'm left looking crazy. Deranged or dumb, in that old sense of the word. And I've caught my reflection of the look before. Disturbing.

I also call her Butt because she's my button. A term of endearment. And let's not forget she's got buttons that make her angry. Ones I admittedly push. Just to push.

She fell for me because of how I talked about not raping her. Explaining this connection between us never comes out right, but I'll give it a shot.

We were having our first date that'd end in sex. That was the deal. A sort of forced agreement. I'd tell her about myself and take her for a ride in my truck if, and only if, we'd get it on. See, already, I sound like an animal. Some macho man trying to show off—then and right now when retelling it. But Betty liked my style, the way I spoke, the way I drove, my muscles, my money. She didn't have a lot of dough. She wouldn't marry for cash and credit (I mean, she was a lone woman who'd gotten by just fine for over fifty years), but she didn't mind the thought. She told me that. And I thought she had an amazing ass. She was fun and nice to talk to, and I wanted to fuck her in that butt.

That was it, right there. She said that that wasn't going to happen. She'd never had butt sex, and she wasn't going to now in her sixties. I assured her it'd be fine, because I'd fucked all sorts of women up the ass. Ha, that's funny, right? It was *then*. She laughed. Next, I said I could prove to her how good it'd feel. She asked how I'd do that. I said, "By fucking you in the butt." She laughed again.

Somewhere in there, it got to consent and being playfully rough. On another date, she put the question out there, asking if I'd raped anyone. "Hell no," I said. "The women who screamed 'don't' or 'stop' loved it." She laughed at that, but it sounded different from the giggles she'd let out earlier. The humor of the topic was a difficult one to sustain. You know how humor can keep a dull conversation going? This was one of those where the funniness was bad but didn't prolong or kill the vibe. The absurdity was too interesting for the both of us.

I apologized and insisted I was a ladies man. I'd had a lot of women but, overall, I was a pleaser.

Being sixty-nine at the time helped those rape jokes. Because rape jokes, as we all know, need all the help they can get to go over well. I'm pretty sure that night I used the number sixty-nine as a gag, too. I also brought up how I'd once followed a supposed rapist in the neighborhood. During my first year as a driver, there were lots of talks about him and his violent deviancy. I used to picture myself squashing the sexual aggressor with my grandpa's truck. I grinned from ear to ear as I relayed the memory to Betty: feeling the squeals of Gramp's tires in my heart, still enjoying the fantasy of flattening that rapist's voice box beneath the Ford F1. She knew my deep truths by that point, first date or no. And, thankfully, people are more accepting of each other when exploring and courting in their sixties.

Am I really going over this first-date scene again? Why? Worried about my own mortality? Because I'll tell ya, I don't usually, if ever, fall into that nonsense—reminiscing.

But, hey, the playback got me here to Bruce's party faster.

"Remember, no drinking."

"What about butt jokes?"

"I don't give a shit," says Betty. She's funny. "But not with a glass in your hand."

"How about a beer?"

"I don't care if you drink beer. What are you, stupid? I mean *hard* liquor. None of it."

No doing butt jokes while drinking the real stuff. Got it.

I should've known that that's what she meant.

I've been getting a little forgetful or literal lately.

But that's okay. What, am I supposed to be surprised by my degenerating? In a month or two, I'll be halfway between seventy and eighty.

CHAPTER 3

Dave's here. Jackson. Mel. Rosey, who's got to be ninety-nine (even though she was a grade under me). Is that Yanni? Hell, I haven't seen him in...I don't know. Months? Years? Fucking wild that I can't narrow down the difference between 30 and 365 days.

I haven't yet set eyes on the Bruce of the hour.

"Lance, where's your drink?" Will asks.

"Wife says I'm a dick if I do," I say.

"Well, do you want to be a hard one or a soft one?"

Is that how *I* sound? I go ahead and laugh with Will, but do I talk like that? He sounds like a frat brat. A drunk punk. A rapist escapist.

Jesus, I've got pussy and ass on the mind. What happened to my main brain occupier—killing people? Let's get back to that, if only because I don't know if I'll have another limp incident when we get home. Because you know Betty's going to want to fuck. Probably doggy-style.

I'm not positive changing the subject from anal sex to murder and back to the ass again is proper preoccupation, but I've now reached thoughts about dogs. How mutts can acquire a taste for human blood if you let them. After the first go, and quenching that temperamental thirst, it's easier for man's best friend to kill and replace all the other friends. Yeah, all you need is some priming. Like anal sex, to come full circle.

"What are you smiling at, Lance?"

Not that anal becomes easier after committing murder.

I wonder, though, if that's the case for the woman. Maybe we need more female murderers out here.

"Lance," Will snaps his fingers and lips. "What the hell are you smiling about?"

"Shit, Will, I'm just grinning, trying to figure out what the hell you meant. You going on about being soft or hard. Are you talking about my dick or my personality?"

"I'd like you to catch up with me on the drinking."

This is weird, because on top of watching that in-shape jogger guy this morning and assuring myself I don't have to keep myself in check when it comes to the comfort level of my sexuality, I've now got Will yapping about soft and hard dicks. And I've already suspected him of being gay. I've known him for over fifty years and always picked him out of the crowd. I'm not saying I'd choose him from a lineup of gays, but he'd be selected as the gay amongst the regular, straight guys. Easily. And he *was* chosen that one time. He's not gay, but someone called him out once. Or tried to for being careless with his words.

I said what I said, asking if he's sizing me up, to make light of what's in my head. To stop picking apart Will's sexual gratifications or homoerotica or whatever.

"I need something to piss on the coals in my eyes," I say. "Put out the fire in my brain."

Will is surprised and laughs as if supercharged.

I also think my overthinking about gayness is me getting used to accepting all kinds. Born after World War II, taking a year between high school and college for myself (the 60's being a confusing time for a white man to do soul searching, society wise), being rejected from the Vietnam lottery draft, not ever going to college, and then watching so many enlist while I sat in complicated self-ridicule. All of that left me not knowing how to be and *especially* leaves me out here with my dick and balls cupped in my fist, not knowing what the fuck to say or how to be today.

There was a time when it was easier to make fun of a

bra burner while slyly relishing the opportunity to titty flick.

Maybe I sound crass. A dirty old man. But I'd counter: maybe I'm a product of a dirty old world, gathering dust on the clearance rack in the corner. Everyone passing by, forgetting there are valuables on that shelf.

I take another drink, wishing this time away, wishing I could fantasize about depopulation (even if by a single person) in peace.

I finish the drink. Another one down.

Sure, I drink alcohol. Hard liquor. Not often, but sometimes, yes.

I'm talking more than I usually do because that's what I do when I drink. Right now, talking about time and the world (mostly America) and what I've seen. And now I'm on the topic of supply and demand. "I demand my supplies," I say. "And I'll get them myself, however I can."

I'm sober enough to ask myself what the hell I'm going on about. I think I'm lecturing. That I'd survive longer than every single person at this function. I think I've insulted my friends, if I had any. I think Betty left me here. She took the car, I've learned, so that means I'm right. Cinches the entirety of my worth. I see this as me being right on all accounts. (Only, Betty would argue these people *do* qualify as friends. She's done it before.)

The last dinner theater we went to (which wasn't one, but sure as hell felt fake as the food, as always, whenever getting dolled up for a fancy round up), right before we left, Betty and I got into a long and loud argument over who truly listens to the other and if we ever really know what the other's going through. I've fucked lots and dated my fair share to know what constituted as good communication, but I wasn't used to so much analytic bull. So I left for that dinner gathering without her, not knowing ditching was a big deal in a relationship. Let's be honest: I knew but didn't give a shit what she did with her night when free booze was involved. I took the long route home, not in any hurry to continue the argument. Inner conflict the entire drive. Wanting to problem wash and get that spice to the throat was my main motivation to show up at the restaurant. When I'd arrived, she was already at the bar, a couple drinks ahead of me (unusual, since she hardly drinks). I quickly apologized before leaving Sober Station. We would make it out alive. She silently agreed which said *something*. For both of us. That was last year, I believe.

"I can walk home," I tell Will, joining him outside with smokers and loudmouths.

Will threatens me to do it. Testing me.

"You think I can't?" I ask him.

I'm unable to match a name to a single face and characterize these six like movie extras: Man #1, #2, #3, #4, #5, and #6. The last of them has his head dropped into the pit of his phone. I want to beat him for owning it. Only, the thing's like a dollhouse glass table. Not satisfying when you want the sound of smacking meat.

"I told you guys," Will says. "Look at his face. Lance's face is always fucked."

"Huh?" I say.

"Smiling like a retard."

Man #3 says, "Don't say that."

Man #6 says, "Say what?"

Man #3 says, "Retard."

They laugh.

Man #1 says, "I get your sense of humor, and I don't want to spoil a good time, but I'll bust your teeth, you say that one more fuckin' time."

Man #4 says, "What?" not grasping Man #1 is serious and has retarded kin.

I say, "Retard?" Because I have a backbone.

Man #1 doesn't know me well enough to touch my teeth, so he glares and says, "Yeah. If everyone has to get it out of their system, then do it now. You've taken your turn, Lance."

Apparently, he and I have met before. Name exchange and everything.

One of Will's goons, in a separate group, waves me away. He's young. Twenty-five. Larger than me. Square. Heavy and maybe has a little muscle beneath his fat.

I get in his face. "You saying something, partner?"

"Walk," speaking for the entire group. "Take a walk, man."

"Fuck you," I say. Hardening my balance, planting my heels.

"You're done," comes from another #.

The one before me repeats this: "You're done."

This is how I make this guy bleed. From his face...

(Making someone bleed from the nose is good. We don't leak from our nostrils unless we're nose bleeders or have a sinus condition or disturb the insides. So, to cause that to happen is a success and empowering. Blood from the ear is usually a rupture and will repair on its own. I think that's what they say about that. I could clap his hearing canals but to produce blood from those holes isn't common nor seen as having/earning a point [in boxing or otherwise]. And people won't bleed from the eyes without a serious tear or broken vessel. That's a horror-movie trick. But to make someone bleed from the face, to bust open the skin, is great. There are cheekbones and gums. Lips and a hairline. A chin, a forehead. But if the flat part of the face splits open, without scratching it, that's fucking terrific.)

What I do after he says, "You're done," as if he's a ref, is bend my knees, dig my heels into my soles, press all of my weight onto the parking lot pavement, punch my fist into the clutch of my other hand, poke out my elbows into a giant arrow like a knight in armor holds his sword to his chest, and wing him in the jaw. I don't miss. I whack him with my wing. I flap his face. You know what I'm saying? I elbow him but in a surprising, sensational way. I clock him one.

I also disturb my rotator cuff. (More about that later, I bet.)

As if strapped to a bomb, I'm cautioned and yelled at. By everyone. Everyone but Will and the guy I hit.

I think they're about to jump me when Will blocks the young men and tells them I'm older than I look. To back off.

I say, "I'll take all you sailors at once!"

Goddamn it, I sound like a fag.

CHAPTER 4

"You broke his jaw, Lance," says Betty. "I can't believe you did that. I can't believe they're not going to press charges or sue."

"Because I'm a pillar."

"A what? Get the hell out of here. No, you're not. He's on parole."

"So you know, then, why he's not pressing charges."

"You shouldn't have drunk, moron." After a couple more minutes of berating me, she says, "We need eggs for the cake," and leaves for the store.

I'm laughing. The entire night's been a riot. Eggs, elbowing, Betty calling me a moron.

Cake?

"Aw, shit," I say, losing the soothing energy of the chuckle. I look to the blank, turned-off television screen and somehow sink lower into the couch. "I forgot."

My cousin, Paul, tried to kill himself. Not recently; a long time ago. Even so, that's his badge of dishonor. His forever stain. He was in a divorce and lost money along with the woman with whom he was having an affair. The hussy had a big nose. That's probably why he tried to off himself. "How could she leave *me* when she's got a schnoz like that?" he cried into a braided rope the color of her hair.

No, he didn't try hanging himself. He took pills like a pussy. I mean that in a couple of ways: pill popping is unceremonious, and that's a woman's way to go out.

I'm looking in a dictionary and reading "unceremonious"

because I can't find "unceremonial," and my laugh comes back like a good friend. Because "unceremonious" can also mean abrupt. And what's suicide if not abrupt?

I don't want to go to another event. Or is the event coming to us?

"Hell," I say, because I'm pretty sure people are coming here. Tomorrow. For Cousin Paul's...birthday? I don't know what the hell the cake is for or for what our house's facilities are going to be used, but I remember Betty talking about hosting.

Did Paul return from fighting in a war? He's a general or a commander. Is he getting remarried? Wasn't he a widow at some point, too?

I don't know anything about him. I know he tried killing himself. I know he doesn't like to talk about it and that everyone else does.

I swear to God, every holiday or family thing someone mentions Paul's attempt. Alluding to it, discussing it, fucking referencing the incident. It was thirty years ago, I think. Maybe twenty. Fifteen at the least. He's over it. Why aren't *we* over it?

I know why, and I'll tell you why: because we don't want to be surprised when he gets it right the next time. We want to say, "I always thought he was still sick," or some crap about him wallowing in self-pity as we self-wallow.

I should fucking kill Paul. Make it look like an accident.

"Fuck me," I giggle, covering my mouth, looking at the nothing television program again. "What if I kill him and set the scene like a botched suicide attempt?"

I'm picturing something like him wanting to jump from a cliff, having a bucket and rope at the ready but leaving the devices at the top of the hill. His broken body at the bottom. Does Jill go tumbling after?

I laugh a little harder. I mean, come on, you have to laugh about the ridiculousness of life sometimes—all the time, if you can. It's like the coyote cartoon fucking up a suicide and the roadrunner bird beep-beeping by at a hundred miles per hour.

I should call Will.

"Hey, man."

"What the fuck, Lance? I don't know what to say. What the fuck?" There's that gayness again in Will's tone.

"I was told not to drink."

"That's a...weak excuse. That was my nephew you hit."

"Why was your nephew at Bruce's thing?"

"Bruce's *retirement* party?"

"Is that what it was?"

"Wes was there because he's probably going to take Bruce's place. Or something else of Bruce's."

"His virginity?"

"Lance, you're a dirty old man, man."

"Is Wes on parole?"

"Wesley?"

"I thought it was Wes."

"What does Wes being on parole have to do with anything?"

"What does Bruce do? Is that a job, what Bruce does? Did?"

"He works for the city and—what is wrong with you? Why'd you call?"

"I don't know, Will. To say that I didn't mean to get blood on your shirt."

"What?"

"It was stupid, me lashing out. I aggravated my rotator cuff."

"Are you kidding?"

"I don't know."

"Because that's not all you aggravated."

"Ha."

"I'm really confused. Are you being serious, Lance?"

"I'm calling because of last night, *Will*."

"I was there. Why are you calling me? You're not—never mind. I'm going to go."

"I didn't mean to drink and do what I did."

"I don't know what that is. I don't know what you're doing. That's a statement. I'll see you in another ten years, fucking jerk."

He ends the call. I smirk. Will's funny. He *is*. What else can I say? Calling me a jerk like a little kid. And ten years? I've probably only seen him a dozen times over the past *twenty* years. He was a friend of a younger brother of someone I balled in high school. We're not buddies. I don't think.

And I don't think Will's gay. That was just me being a paranoid geezer in this particular day and age, a time where my suspicions tend to stand out more.

What the hell does "day and age" mean? I know what it means, but when we say "this day and age," we're referring to the past while pretending to talk about the present. That's it. Nothing else. The past we know. The past we read about. The past we were taught. Accurate, inaccurate, half-listened to, fabricated from so many sources. Especially nowadays. And then we relate it to today? That doesn't make sense.

I like "nowadays" better. It assesses the past while regulating something more. A day and an age is too much of something for us to claim to understand.

This day? This age? Nah. That's a full-of-shit concept. Nowadays is the here and now, still relating it to the past.

Nowadays, I'm confused as a son of a bitch. A basic comparison: how I used to understand stuff versus today.

See how that's better? And it's an honest fucking statement, too. Because, lately, I *am* confused as a son of a bitch. Not about what gets my dick up and hard but–or is it hard and up?

I think I'm ruminating about my ability to concentrate and process, which may question how much confidence I truly have and can hold on to on a daily basis, but that's only because I'm being honest with myself when thinking about my looks. My appearance.

Damn, how women loved me.

That jogger from earlier or yesterday–I wonder if he knows what he's got. Does he have any idea how to hold onto it–his body, his heart, his stamina, his purpose? Does he know what he's doing on that sidewalk? Why he's there?

You know what you're going to do, Lance? You're going to sit outside your porch every day until you catch the bastard. You're going to strike him with a conversation.

"Did you call him?" Betty asks, shouting over her opening and shutting cupboards, putting away the groceries.

"Yep. Are you making pork chops tonight?"

"You apologized?"

"Yep."

She's a goddamn psychic. How does she do that? She doesn't know me well enough. She doesn't know me at all, if you want me to be truthful about our relationship. But reading people's dos and don'ts, and predicting behaviors, and getting in my mind gives me the willies.

"What are you smirking about over there?" she asks.

"The willies."

"What?"

"Did you get potatoes?"

"Potatoes?"

"Stop splashing the bags around and maybe you could hear me, Butt."

"*Splashing*?"

"I don't know," I say, ornery and resentful as a long-haired traveler with a skinny dog at his grubby feet. "That plastic sound."

"It gives you the willies?"

"No, you dumb butt. *You* give me the willies. And that's funny, because I called Will. Willies."

She's not saying anything.

"You hear me?" I ask.

"Uh-huh."

"Not funny? Not interesting?"

"Not particularly."

"Well, go die."

She stops. That was a hard button I just pushed.

"Excuse me?" she says, standing upright, making full eye contact like a tiger for prey.

"What?" I sound scared. Fuck that. "What?!"

"Don't shout at me."

"What are you looking at?"

"A dirty old man."

"Shut up."

"And *go die*?"

I don't feel regret. I just want her to stop looking at me. So I say, "I'm sorry."

"No. No, no, Lance. What the hell is wrong with you that you think you can say something like that to me? I'm your wife. You're supposed to love me. And care for me."

"Aw, hell."

"No! You don't treat people like that."

"*Treat*? I just said some words."

"And the ones you chose, the order you said them, and how you directed them to me–"

Oh shit, I'm back to laughing. I cover my mouth. Again, I say, "I'm sorry."

"Fuck you, Lance," she says, quietly, angrily. "Fuck you," she repeats, gently, damaged.

"It was funny how you said I put my words in a certain order...hey...Butt?"

The bedroom door cuts me off. No slam. Just a lonely click.

I snort.

And after reading a junk mail flier for about a half an hour, I wonder if Betty's dead. Did she kill herself in the bedroom? I don't think there's anything in there to do the job. Could she have climbed out the window? At sixty-nine? I think she's in good enough shape to do that.

I'm not sure why I said it. I haven't really gone over what I said this entire time, now sitting and scanning the newspaper for pictures and ads. I'm not sure I can remember what I said.

Was it *Shut the fuck up*? *Get out of here*? *Go get fucked*? Oh. *Go get fucked and die*. No. *Go on and die*. Along those lines. Yeah, the death thing. Telling her to *die already*. More or less.

I don't want to sit in the dark this evening and wonder if I should or shouldn't turn on the living room lamp. Also, I'd have to close the bedroom windows, where she is, to turn on the central air. Because it feels like it's heating up tonight. I for sure don't want to sacrifice my comfort, debating over what is right or wrong (to turn on the central air or not). I can't go through that tonight. Too much has happened since yesterday. I'm going to make peace.

"Hey, Butty?" (Which sounds like "buddy.") "Are you awake?"

She's asleep.

Perfect. I'll close the bedroom windows, leave her alone, close the bedroom door behind me, and turn on the air.

I'd like to watch *The A-Team* tonight. Or *Airwolf* with Ernest Borgnine. Something silly and memorable.

First, I'm going to go out and buy myself a malt milkshake. And I have to remember not to stay up too late. That jogger should be making his way past our house around 9:00 a.m.

CHAPTER 5

Two days. Nothing followed by nothing. I get my ass out there on the front porch and sit with a newspaper, or trim a bush, or fight the desire or physical need to doze off from 7:45 to 11:00 a.m. and have a whole lot of nothing to show for my nothingness.

I get a snack and start watching for the jogger from the window. Right away, I get a cramp in my neck. All that leaning and turning to check the sidewalk.

Having a stakeout inside a house really gets you hating the walls. So you go back outside. And then back in. Repeat. Repeat. All the way until noon, I do this. For nothing. All this work for just nothing. Nothing for nothing.

Betty comes out. I sigh.

"What's up, grumpy?" she asks.

"I'm thinking of golfing."

"Since when?"

"Since when? What does that mean?"

"I mean, you don't golf."

"I'm not golfing now. And when I do, I'll be golfing then."

"What are you talking about, Lance?"

"Golfing!"

"But what—of course you're not golfing now in the house...never mind."

"I'm talking about me swinging a golf club. Something I'll do nowadays."

"Nowadays?"

"Uh-huh."

"I'm not confused as to—why *golf* of all things, I'm asking, bonehead? When you have hip problems. Golf is all about twisting."

"Twisting the night away."

"You're so weird sometimes."

Ever since the night I told Betty—asked her, advised her, ordered her—to die, I've been thinking about how she will come to her demise. Will it be a fall? A break-in gone wrong? A bug sting during a Bahamas trip? I know she's going to die before me. She has to. I have too much to live for.

"And there's that shit-eating grin on your face again, too," she says.

"Who the hell eats shit and then grins about it?"

"Someone who's guilty for eating it. Loving the pleasure of sneaking shit from a toilet."

"Jesus, Betty, you're disgusting."

Now, she's grinning. The shit's contagious.

We're a couple of old cooks. Crazy old timers in a middle-class neighborhood. Maybe she'd be interested in my thoughts about killing. She can usually hold her end of a strange topic for longer than most.

"We should watch some Hitchcock movies," I say.

"When? Tonight?"

"Don't tell me we have another party to host or go to."

"You hardly attended the last one. What would you care if we did?"

"I wouldn't."

"No, we aren't hosting tonight, dummy."

The work I had to put into avoiding everyone that night. Birthday-cousin Paul and the rest of them. I didn't want to hear about his suicide attempt, his successes, or for whatever reason everyone was coming to our place. Leave me alone. Get out of my house. I don't like any of you, you don't like me. The so-called guests don't lend recognition, acceptance, or eye contact. Not one eyeball counts me in. And I don't give a shit. Not one shit, nor two shits for these people. I'd love to forget every one of you.

Mutual meandering around the room is stupid as hell anyway. Lifeless facial expressions. Idiotic conversation topics. Wishy-washy bullshit. And no drinking to dampen and soften it all (wife's orders). It's a house-arrest party. The jail cell following me around like a Halloween costume. An invisible tether that resembles my hairy testicles snuggly snapped inside my wife's change purse. Might as well be a costume party. We *do* all wear masks at these things, correct?

I might not have known what in God's name the party was truly about, but I can say it gave my family multiple opportunities to illustrate how much more they like Betty than me. I was cloaked in shit with a shitty expression and shitty ideas before the fifteen to twenty family members ever arrived to shit in my toilet.

"Down the hall and on the right," I said once, lying.

How hilarious is that? I live here and gave the wrong directions to the only toilet in the house. The cousin-in-law's kid, or whatever he was, getting turned around wasn't what made it funny. The idea of me not knowing the location of my own bathroom or, even better, dishing out inaccurate directions on purpose is what almost got me spitting out my sparkling water. I can be a jokester but not to *that* extent. Playing pranks isn't normally my style. I'm more of a regular well-ain't-that-a-shame, sarcastic-expression person. Does that make sense? I don't think it would've made sense to explain myself to any of those family people. Like that guy who stood confused for probably a good ten seconds before realizing I didn't mean for him to piss in the closet. He wouldn't have got me.

"Lance," another family member called out, proving he remembered me, sticking me in a state of competitiveness. I didn't take it as a swing or a jab. I kept on keeping on– watching fights instead of starting them. I promised Betty.

"No throwing any elbows," I whispered to this guy, in a way, a continuation of withholding verbal abuse as I had been for the past forty to forty-five minutes.

"Thank you so much," said the mocking bastard. Tossing my name and exiting my residence. Fine by me. Get your cold one from the fridge and get out.

It was around that time I looked through the window and spotted Will outside. I'd forgotten he was there. Invited or stopping by? I now can't recall.

Will's supposed to be setting me up for a "meet-and-greet" to work at a record store (a vinyl shop). Will's also the one who secured my first job as a car salesman. He's all right. He's probably a good friend. He accepts me, and I don't show appreciation. I could be better at that. Some other time.

Another twelve to fifteen minutes of uninterrupted indoor time passed before Will stole my sparkling water, cracked open a Faygo, and gently placed it in my hand. I sipped. Not a minute later, Will slapped me on the back.

"Mm-hm," I said in place of "stop." Slurping—a defense mechanism Betty's mentioned.

"What's that there? A cold Fag-o."

"You handed it to me."

"Yeah? You accepting dicks, too?"

"Were you raped by your coach or what?"

Will's face did a dance, and the reaction was not satisfying. I think he was pitying my outburst, if that makes sense. Or was I pitying him, trying to associate his absurdity with a pinch of his trauma?

Freshman year of high school, I was almost molested by our football coach. I exaggerate, but not really. No one knew. No one *knows*.

There were rumors the coach was the asshole-poking type before I arrived to high school, but they would have died down by the time Will got there. (Goddamn, anyone ever investigate anything back then?) In that short time, he'd already unsuccessfully tried working his perverted version of fag magic on me and received an elbow to the gut. How weird that a moment like that is filed under being tested as a man.

I know, nowadays, you're not supposed to think of gays and perverts as synonymous, and I really try not to. I guess it's just in my nature to want to kill somebody who threatens me. Not as if there's a danger revolving around my sexual orientation, but it's me and what I do when being cautious of my asshole. I used to envision beating that coach with an abandoned golf club I glimpsed in the high school rec room. I'm sure my distrust of homosexuals comes from Coach Debaucher abusing his power. But am I threatened by two homos going at it? No. I need to remember that. Continue working on it. My 21st-century goal. I'll make an effort to accept terrorists in the 22nd. (Not that they're equally threatening. Hating that I have to justify that thought to myself.) Will's about eight years younger than me, and the coach left my junior year, so he wouldn't remember the guy.

In my face, Will said, "My nephew was supposed to be here tonight."

"You're an asshole, Will," I belched. "You act like you're not, but you're just as bad as me. Was there supposed to be a fight for everyone to watch? Me and your nephew? What's his name again?"

I concentrated on the fight on TV, floundering in the connection I'd just made, wondering if I was being witty or lazy.

"First: you're an old man," Will said. "You're his age times three. So, no. My idea wasn't to get the two of you to scrap. At your house? No way, man. Second: I wanted you all to settle yourselves, because he's an investor. Or manager. I'm not sure, but he has a hand in that record store. The vinyl shop. The vinyl store."

"Will I be working with your nephew? What's his name?"

"No. He's a silent partner or getting permits figured out for the land the record store sits on. Bruce is the one who had the connections to the building in the first place."

"You don't know shit about any of it."

"My nephew's on parole, or used to be, and he's straightening up. Or out. Whichever. A lot of business sense."

"If he has any sense, it's more than I can say for you."

"Hey, I keep relationships with difficult people. Why else would I still be talking to you after all these years?"

"Whose kid is he? Your brother's?"

"No."

"How does your nephew know me? Through Bruce? What's his fuckin' name?"

"City cliquey stuff. He knows you helped out with coaching and supports that about you. Recognizes the one good thing you've done with your life."

Coaching. Was that a coincidence? Was I purposely unburying some hate there? Differentiating? Gays vs. pedophiles? If I was, good for me.

"I was only an assistant coach," I said. "And I haven't done that deed since before I met Betty."

Will probably said more. I'd stopped listening by this point and returned to my list.

Throughout the shindig, I was entertaining myself by jotting down movie titles. Those trippy ones with the commas and/or question marks. Unusual, intriguing, and some of them long as hell.

Currently reviewing the sheet, I recall grouping them according to themes, now forgetting the themes:

It's a Mad, Mad, Mad, Mad World
Dr. Strangelove or: How I Learned to Stop Worrying and Love the Bomb
The Good, the Bad and the Ugly
They Shoot Horses, Don't They?
The Last House on the Left
The Little Girl Who Lives Down the Lane
Assault on Precinct 13
Everything You Always Wanted to Know about Sex* (*But Were Afraid to Ask)

When a Stranger Calls
Sorry, Wrong Number
Who's that Knocking at My Door?
Whatever Happened to Baby Jane?
Who is Harry Kellerman and why is He Saying Those Terrible Things about Me?
Who's Afraid of Virginia Woolf?

The Texas Chain Saw Massacre
License to Kill
Kiss Me Deadly
Night of the Living Dead
I Spit on Your Grave

Lock, Stock, and Two Smoking Barrels and *Dude, Where's My Car?* inspired the 21ˢᵗ century's first ten years of movie titles, allowing all sorts of vampire flick-like titles. *There Will Be Blood* started them off again some years later. But I didn't write down newer movies.

Deeper in the evening, Will had dove headfirst into a drunken state. He snatched the list off of the end table and read, his inhibitions to dismiss such an out-of-character act gone. (Because to feign interest is not Will's style.)

"It reads like a poem," he said. Slowly, he set the sheet down and patted it like the top of a dedicated dog's skull. I learned, then, that Will's a quiet, pleasant drunk. I believe he respected the list.

I currently reread the titles and agree; it's like a poem. The subconscious has laid itself out like a dark, dark plan of attack for the future. Better pocket this or commit it to memory.

"Which one?"

"Huh?" I say, sounding like a babbler in hospice. "Which what?"

"Which Hitchcock movie?" Betty asks, forcing me to the present as only a wife knows how. "I like *Psycho*."

"Yeah, that's good. Me, too. But what about something with more talking? Discussions about the murders and crimes."

"Okay," she says with that modern non-agreement, not-understanding-an-oddball-request tone. "Um...*Rear Window*? Well, that goes back and forth. They talk and then they look out the window."

"What about *Shadow of a Doubt*?"

"I don't care, Lance. Honestly."

"How do I get it?"

"I don't know. TV?"

"TV? Betty, what does that–I said 'how.' *TV*?"

"You asked me."

"I don't understand you sometimes."

"You sound like Oliver Hardy. Do *you* have any bright ideas?"

"On *how*? No. But I can think of something better than *TV*."

She stops folding the towels and looks at me, studying my face. "You're being mean again."

"I'm sorry," quick as an elbow reflex, so we can move past the ancient banter and figure out how to get the movie up and running. I'll make popcorn for a change. "I'm laughing. That's all."

"Can I ask you something?" she says, back to folding.

"Yes, babe."

"Hardy called Laurel babe?"

"Yes, bitch?"

"Funny," she says, straight as a comedian. "Could you not laugh at my expense?"

I laugh. To fuck with her.

I say, "You first."

She squeezes my hand, lovingly. Her digs truly are different than mine.

Halfway through the movie, I get the courage to say, "This is better than I remembered."

There's this omen in the movie world: if you compliment a film out loud, that review will immediately ring false and all moving parts will fail. It's a sure thing. You can enjoy your time. Make faces at each other. Silently comment on your appreciation. But if you specifically state, "The music is powerful," the next blowing, brass horn of the musical score will tickle your embarrassment. "I'm surprised how good he is in a serious role," comes out, and the thespian's acting chops quickly scramble mid-facial reaction.

Simply put: you jinx it.

And the second half of *Shadow of a Doubt* is no different and no good. Theory proven.

"Well, that was a fucking disappointment," I say in my best impression of a nasty, crotchety version of Oliver Hardy.

Betty laughs and pops out her tit.

We're bonkers, right?

Throughout sex (lots of rubbing, caressing, holding) and still this morning, I'm thinking of how I could lure Betty into joining me for a talk about cold-blooded murder. I'm reviewing my options when I see the jogger three blocks down.

My brain scans my cock to see if there's any movement. Of course there's not. But it's that old (young) masculine side of me that has to make sure I'm not in denial or repressed by the God-fearing 1950's.

Nope. My dick's as soft as chewed bubblegum, and I'm as straight as an arrow.

I get to the porch. As he passes, I say, "Keep that up."

He stops. Not wearing headphones. That's a surprise.

"What's that?" he asks with a smile. He looks confused.

"Oh, I was just saying to keep at it. I used to be fit like you. Half a life ago. I'm still up to it. *At* it, I mean. Doing what I can."

"That's awesome," he says, to what, I haven't a clue. "How have you adapted?"

"What? Oh, I'm fine. Moving along. I'm seventy-four."

"Okay."

"You're supposed to say, 'You look good for your age.'"

"You do. I was thinking that."

"My wife tells me not to do that. I'm not fishing."

"I thought you were, yeah, younger than that."

I look fifty-nine. I know that. I've been told that, and I know that. Maybe sixty-two, but it's easier to think of myself at the end of my fifties. And I'm sure it's easier, what others see as kinder, for them to put me at the end of my fifties. But truthfully, I can look fifty-five a good six times out of the year. These last few years, I've definitely pulled off fifty-five. Sunglasses and a beard sometimes helps.

"Keep it up. Like I said," I say. "Because having the body is everything." I look to see if Betty can hear. She's deep in the house, awake and busy. "I'm not bragging or–I kept in shape. And that kept the ladies after me."

He laughs. I think to agree. But fuck him. I don't need his approval and secret ridicule.

"That's why I asked how you're adapting," he repeats. "You know, where you find satisfaction in different things."

I don't know what the hell he's talking about.

"Oh yeah," I say, "I'm fine. And, like I said, keep at it. That body's the only one you've got."

"Got it," he says, starting to jog in place like a giant toy. "I'll see you around."

"I'm sure you will," I say. I don't know what the fuck I mean by it.

The two of us made no goddamn sense. What was the point of that interaction?

I get inside, channeling a grouchy disposition into something else, a conversation I want, and say to Betty, "What's the reason we talk to strangers?"

"Oh, man," she says, sighing, doing something–always something–to the items of our house. "What now?"

"Never mind."

"No, Lance, I'm just worried about ya. You've been so up and down lately."

"What's *lately*?"

"Forget it. What were you going to say?"

"Strangers. We talk to them to, what, to make new friends? Learn something about them? Ourselves?"

"Maybe all of that. Why not?"

"What compels us?"

"Loneliness. Or maybe we're in a good mood."

"What if we're in a bad mood?"

"Yeah, we reach out. I don't get your meaning."

"What if we want to get something off of our chest?"

"*Chests*."

"What?"

"It'd be getting something off all of our chests," she says. "Which doesn't sound very peace-loving. A bunch of people complaining."

"*Peace-loving*? Where do you come up with these?"

I feel threatened. It's an old punch to the ribs or pinch of the nipple. A lingering threat from hippies. Back then, I'd pray they'd try to jump me. Knowing they were too wrapped in peace-loving to do anything as simple as connecting a punch. And then, how Charles Manson's approach had intrigued me. Exposing the capabilities and buried aggression that was in that long-haired community all along.

I say, "We should rent another Hitchcock movie."

"That's fine with me," she says, walking away and toward another part of the house that apparently needs her attention. "As long as it doesn't take long to get it going."

"Are you saying I took a long time to put the movie on last time? Or something else?"

She laughs.

I later pick *Dial M for Murder* from the library. Day leaks out to night. The movie ends by eight o'clock. We switch from the movie-source input back to TV programming. It takes about five to six minutes. There aren't many awkward silences inside our marriage, but we have one now.

We're not discussing the film. We're not ready for bed. Neither of us is horny. Volume's low on the set.

"What do you think about killing someone?" I ask. After a Hitchcock movie, you can jump right in. Easy.

"Uh, that you'll go to jail."

"I know, but like someone having to kill because they're blackmailed. Or a person might go to jail if someone squeals on them."

"*Squeals*?" She raises her eyebrows and chuckles.

"Do you think you could?"

"Kill? No. Out of self-defense, yes. I wouldn't repeatedly hit someone till they died if I knew I was safe or had the chance to leave, but—"

"But what about *that*? In the movies, they never do that. The person gets away from the murderer or the murderer is dead. For certain. Someone comes in and saves the day, shoots the bad guy, or the bad guy falls off a cliff. Something along those lines. But what if you were in a confined space and had to end the guy's life?" I can't help but look around the room, judging our distance from the windows and walls and exits and the phone. "If you hit the intruder, the killer, and he's not unconscious, and you don't have time to get away, or maybe you're in the desert, and he'll find you, even if you have a full minute head start. Could you do it?"

"Keep hitting him? I don't know. No. I'd call for help or hide. I don't know."

"That's stupid. Listen. I just said you could be in a desert."

"Don't call me stupid."

"I said, '*That's* stupid.'"

"And I said *that*, so maybe don't call my answer stupid."

"Alright, Betty, but I don't think that would be very wise. To hide when you have a killer in the house, or are in the basement of a factory, somewhere where you can't get help. You'd hide?"

"I'd get a weapon."

"Like what? A fireplace poker? A kitchen knife?"

"Maybe."

"What about that? Could you stab someone? Over and over?"

"If we were in a struggle."

"Where would you stab him?"

"How close are we, this killer and I? Physically?"

"If I were to get on you–" I stand and approach. She backs into the couch cushion. "What are you doing?"

"What are *you* doing?"

"I'm not going to hurt you."

"I know."

"What the hell, Betty? You don't have a knife."

"No. I don't." What's *that* mean?

"Forget it," I say, disappointed in being unable to rehearse a murder.

"I think I'm feeling funny from the movie," she says, not knowing what the hell she's feeling. Like me.

"I'm not wanting to scare you, Butt. I was curious."

"I know," she says, straightening up, locking into proper posture, acting as if we're having a jolly old time after a pleasant, friendly Hitchcock viewing. "I think..." I watch her circling her thoughts, homing in on which words sound natural, questioning how to make them a part of our Normal. Like we've retracted the projector screen to discuss Communism takeovers. "I don't think I'd be able to stab him over and over," she says. "If he were attacking me and wouldn't stop, sure. But even that sounds tiring."

"You could stab him in the head or face," I say. Smiling. Hoping I don't appear shadowed and murderous.

She laughs, just as embarrassed as our first date. "I don't know, Lance. It's a hard scenario to picture."

Good. She's achieved her end of normalcy. Which

means so have I. "I'm only wondering."

"Could you do it?" she asks. "Kill someone for something that'd constitute as your survival?"

"Constitute?"

"Yeah. Do you want to look up the word before you answer?"

"Feisty little cunt, are we?"

"Hey. Jesus."

Again, that dropdown face of hers. Is this a new mask or a mask-slip due to her age?

"What?" I ask, guilty as hell.

"I was kidding," she says.

"Fuck. Okay."

"Watch your mouth."

"I can fucking swear."

"That's not what I'm talking about, Lance."

"I was joking, too. We both were."

"But you have a jab in your voice sometimes, and that's the third time you've done it."

"You're keeping count of my insults? I'd be at twenty if I counted yours."

"I'm sorry if I do that."

"Jabbing me just as often."

"Not like that, Lance. You know what I'm talking about. It's your tone."

"To hell with my tone."

"You going to elbow me in the jaw next?"

"Maybe."

Oops. She leaves me for the bedroom. And, damn it, the windows are open and it's another hot one tonight. She'll be under the ceiling fan. No turning on the central air. For me, no cooling off.

CHAPTER 6

I spied on my neighbors when I was younger. And I mean multiple neighbor *homes* when I say "neighbors." Multiple women. Multiple girls. Multiple times of my life. I was a boy when they were girls. I was a boy when they were women. I was a man when they were women.

I moved around a lot as a kid. Seven homes before I was ten years old.

For some reason, how my memory saves it, or luck, I was surrounded by beautiful females every move. Across the street. Next door. The apartment upstairs. The apartment across the hall. Visiting mothers. Visiting friends. Visiting relatives. The three who worked at the deli at the end of the block.

Most of the time, I was too young to date. They were five years older or double my age. When I was a young man, the distance and obstacles prevented me from striking up conversations. They didn't jog, those women. Not yet. And even if jogging had been a pastime back then, there's no way I'd have had the courage to approach a woman as I did with that jogger from our neighborhood. I've gotten bolder in my later years. Too bold, it seems, because Betty hasn't spoken to me for two full days since my cutting words.

I haven't returned to these memories to defend my basic peeping-Tom rights, but do realize I've been conditioned over time to justify myself. Haven't I? Isn't that what I'm doing? Making excuses for a natural, horny childhood? How I'm a man. How I'm not a pervert. How

I'm a guy who's nice enough and smart enough. To gain some recognition. I should be enough.

Instead, I grow tired, feeling I have to take the blame for not doing enough for others. And I don't *have* to do anything for others. I'm managing through life like everybody else. Not depressed or searching for meaning. A little bored, I'll admit. But very fucking exhausted by the nonsense I've put up with.

I'm sure some of the things I see as tedious absurdities are the buttons Betty wears. And I'm also aware those buttons have been pressed pretty hard by me, probably sticking the last couple of our five years together.

But, hey, you don't want me to respond a certain way? Too bad. Too fucking bad for you. Because I'm retired, babe. I've dealt with life and finally, after all these years, have a chance to sit back and think about that bucket list everyone talks about. Somewhere between my current state–volunteering when the mood strikes, taking care-free drives, being offered and accepting and becoming accustomed to free books and meals and senior discounts and geriatric pity for less than ten years–there's a list to make to contest despair.

It needs to be filled or checked off.

And, Betty, between you and me, sometimes there are pretty young ladies about (and by young, I mean thirty or forty...or twenty years old). And you should know whenever I think of talking to them, I accept how truly retired I am, especially from getting involved in nonsense arguments. I've been retired from that kind of work for some twenty years, and refuse to go back and improve upon my social skills as if I'm a fucking case study for the old. I don't need additional, outside pressure to be self-analytical and ashamed. I'm going to have some goddamn purpose with or without y'all. (The eyes of my reflection reveal how badly I hate convincing myself of a point, especially when no one else is around to blame for my self-loathing.)

"You know, Butt," I start off, not twenty feet from her, "I think you being sixty-nine puts me at an advantage." I'm roughly thirty feet away. We've got a big backyard. I'm a sneaky, fighting son of a bitch for getting into this talk from such a distance. It's a trick where I present as if I'm at a disadvantage and vulnerable but am, in fact, catching her off guard and putting her in a position to work a little harder at listening and talking from the physical space I maintain.

"I can't hear you," she says.

I'm trying to be on top. It's not working, and it's pissing me off. I bet she *can* hear me but won't.

Feeling like the poked bear or a frightened elephant or the brain of some blood-sniffing shark, I attempt to continue my outskirts attack with some truth. "Betty, I'm sorry," and carefully phrase, "for coming at you from a darker place. Ever since–"

"I still can't hear you."

"Goddamn it." I get closer and, although I'm aware of it, don't fully understand how my ploy to irritate her has backfired. "I said–can you hear me?"

"What?" like she knows what I was doing all along.

"I think I've been talking to you from a low place, and I apologize for you being the one there, taking my crap."

"You've been rude. And I sometimes react harshly."

"I don't want my mean streak to ruin our summer."

"So, then, give it rest, okay? Please?" She hasn't once taken her eyes away from the tomato plants. She's winning this one. I'll give it to her. I have to give the excuse, though. That bit of truth that's like a kernel in the gums.

I say, "Ever since I was shot down by that college-registration idiot–"

"I've told you, they can't turn you away," she says, looking up at me and the sunlight but ultimately diverting her eyes. "They want your money."

"It was *free* for senior citizens."

"Registration fees not included. And you can't go fulltime. And that registration idiot never gave us a straight answer, whether that included getting a master's or not. She was an imbecile."

"She was a fucking dumbass."

"She was. Saying you're too old."

"That's not what she said, but—"

"She was saying you're too old. Oh, she can go screw herself. She knew what she was saying. That's what she meant."

This is the Betty I fell in love with. This is the woman that's on my side. Another "me" for myself.

"And I get it," she continues. "You're not going to become a professor after getting a Ph.D., and how that'd put you at, what, over eighty years old? With no experience except what you'd do during your internship and dissertation?" I'm suddenly feeling worse, especially because she is putting all of this in the form of a question. "But that doesn't mean you might not enjoy yourself by learning some new things." Who gives a damn about that? "Meeting new people. Everyone gets something out of meeting someone new. It's how we get on."

That's true. But do I have to pay college course prices for that?

"And you'd be contributing," Betty continues, gardening in a calmer, more concise manner than when I first arrived. "Your thoughts. Your time. Everyone benefits from talking."

"I don't want to talk about it."

"You brought it up."

"But now I feel shittier."

"I'm not trying to make you feel worse."

"But I do feel worse. It's not you. It's the facts of my situation."

"What's your situation?"

"That I want to do something different."

"Go ahead. You could be around another twenty-five years. They might have advances in medicine and a way to prolong life. We don't know. Maybe you'll live out the rest of your life on the moon."

Sort of farfetched, but maybe. Technology changes the world overnight. I just don't like how Betty sometimes talks about my future without her in it. She doesn't notice she does it. And, frankly, I don't give a shit if she is in my future or not. If she sees herself as moving on and growing in another man's arms or with less arguing, she can have at it. I just don't like the idea of not knowing where I am in the future.

I walk away, not sure why I entered the hottest spot of the yard in the first place. I don't want your opinions. I don't need you to reflect my bitterness. I'll shove that knife out into the world when I want. Leave me the fuck alone.

I step into a hare hole.

CHAPTER 7

"A nest of kittens," says Betty, I swear to God, flirting with the doctor.

"That's cute," he says.

"But they were rabbits," I say.

I want to stand and "find my footing," as they say. But I'm unable. My hip's been plucked and fucked like a goddamn virgin. I eyeball the doc through my glasses.

Why the hell am I still wearing these? I stopped reading in the waiting room over thirty minutes ago.

"So," I say. "Surgery or not?"

He says we'll see after some tests, or physical therapy, or x-rays. I don't listen. I'm wondering what would be the best instrument to end this lab coat's days. I'd have to keep Betty quiet. I wouldn't need an instrument for her. Just some sweet talking.

What got me going on this murder-fantasy spree was that day at the college and the nightmare I had the night before.

On campus, in one of the many offices, I scanned a pamphlet for some modern-hippie club bullshit which got me thinking of the hate we have in the world. Is there more of it than before? More advertisements of our anger? Can raising awareness be self-defeating? Has our definition of hate changed within this last century? All the "isms" of the world—what's behind them? I was going over these types of thoughts about society, and where we are every hundred years, and massive death counts, when I was slammed by that registration bitch with the textbook ageism. This world runs on an ageist attitude. The hate of being old. The hate of witnessing our mortality in others' wrinkly faces. Stuff I'd overheard a flock of sheep bleating about ten minutes earlier.

I say, embrace the gravity and diseases and deterioration and fuck off with your clock.

Men are beginning to date older women? This is progressive? No, it's happening because of the advancements in makeup and hairstyles and exercises. Women have learned how to look younger for longer. A sixty-year-old woman without facelift bucks can still appear as a sexy forty. Late thirty-year-olds can party with early twenty-year-olds. And men look like boys, polished and prancing in stylish clothing. Not until year twenty-eight does today's hunk finally look mature enough to move out and pay a bill. The forty-year-old female hottie with the little-girl pigtails, on the other hand, looks like she was on the same yearbook page as the immature man-boy going on thirty. And now smokin'-hot women in their sixties and seventies are going to get in the sack with twenty-year-old studs. No protection needed.

So no, people, we're not getting better or more accepting. We're nonstop faking it for sex. We want to stick it in or be the one getting stuck or rub all we can with the healthy. We want to fuck as a people, as a world. And we're mad and ashamed when we can't.

I, personally, don't want to be in that world. I don't ever think I was for that kind of planet. I'm more than that. I'm more than you. That's *one* reason to kill them all.

The other factor that rolled this idealistic killing along was that nightmare. How crazy, motivation was lying there in my subconscious for years. Killing off three people in a dream. I'm sure it was symbolic. But the big change-a-roonie for me was feeling so goddamned good when I awoke. I shouldn't call it a nightmare. It was more of an enlightening experience.

Doc leaves. The door clicks.

Betty smirks.

"What?" I say, knowing what.

"You."

"I'm not jealous."

"Alright, Lance."

"You were just acting like a slut."

There I went again. And she leaves me in the room.

What the hell did the doctor say? Am I waiting here or good to go? I need Betty to recap.

I open the door. She's gone. I wait for her to return, unknowingly giving her time to continue down the hall and enter the lobby where she'll win the wait-out contest.

After about twenty minutes of wandering like Elmer Fudd, I say, "Excuse me," to a nurse, remembering it's impossible for me to get over how fuckable women are today. More so than the miniskirt days of the 60's even. They're not as free and available, but they're all pinup girls or magazine-layout material. "Am I waiting for something?"

She doesn't look at me when she says, "Yep, you'll be having x-rays." And the bitch leaves. She treats me like an old creep. She assumed I'd eye-fuck her. She assumed I was slow, processing like an older gentleman on my way to dementia and, next stop, Grave Terminal. She knew, somehow, I'd be confused or impatient. And I'm not up for that. Not this guy. Not today. Not this fucking year. *You're* the predictable one.

Recently, it had to have been within the past year, the same week I had the dream, I saw on some show the theory of there being three main motives to kill: money (some kind of gain—status, land), love (jealousy, possession, and more), or revenge (based on pride or taking a stand against something challenging your ego). Theoretically, a murder motive falls under one of these categories, more or less. In my dream, however, I didn't have any of those aims. It just felt good as hell to end another's life.

I follow the nurse two rooms down from mine.

"Excuse me, nurse."

She does an appalled, "Ex*cuuuuse* me," as if I'd smacked her hiney.

"I didn't hear you," I pretend.

"You can't be in here."

"I'm deaf in one of my ears. I forget which one."

"Sir, I will be with you in a moment."

"I just want to know if my table's ready."

I screwed that up. I said the line too clearly. I should have slurred. Now, she knows I'm being a hard ass. Man, she has a hard ass.

Briefly, I entertain myself, thinking of masturbating as I await her return.

Sorry 'bout that, hon. I'm senile. Duh?!

I think better of it, go back to my room, and look around with fierce eyes. No one notices. No one to see. It's a ghost hall. Once, occupied; now, trapped souls (whether the patients have died of waiting, cancer, or a diagnosis).

I'm not waiting. I refuse my prognosis and the x-ray.

"Lance?"

"That's my first name."

"We're all set."

A different sexpot. Fine. I'll hop after this cottontail down the radiation rabbit hole instead.

Why the fuck am I so horny? I'm going to have an erection just as they place me on the cold table with the giant robot. I'll develop a tumor on the tip of my prick. Poking out and over the lead blanket like a sneaky snake.

"How are you doing today?" she asks, her voice at that bang-me-any-day pitch.

"Following you? I'm swell...ing."

She doesn't look back. No disgust. No interest. I don't think she listened to my answer. I don't think she gives a shit. Nothing for nothing.

"I asked for a booth," I say, really going for the inappropriate old-timer role, sticking charm in a bucket of poop.

"Your server will be right with you," she matches.

I'm so fucking close to smacking her ass on the way out. The only reason I don't is because I can't decide if it should be light, hard, or a grip. And the moment passes.

"I need hip surgery," I end up telling Will over the phone. "Or a replacement. Something like that."

"I heard you got kicked out," he says, ignoring my ailment. I've become accustomed to speaking to Will once every other year, but sometimes I wish I knew how to complain and be heard.

"Who said that? Betty Butt? She was jealous of the poon and puss there, is all. I'll tell ya, I could've bent a couple of those scrubs over the operating table if I were so inclined."

"Operating table?"

"Forget it."

"Scrubs?" Will laughs. First time in a week he gets me. I swear, my lashing out at Bruce's retirement gig has gotten us closer. "Is that derogatory?" he asks.

"To call someone a scrub? It's dirty. I like it."

He laughs again. We're officially making up, I think.

"I'll make amends with your nephew," I say. "He can fight me when I have my cast on. Make it fair."

"You don't get a cast on your hip unless it's broken, dumbass. Did you get kicked out of the hospital or not?"

"Practically. But it wasn't cinematic enough to shoot."

"I don't know what you're talking about. Ever."

"No one grabbed me or escorted me out. I didn't lose my mind inside some glass room."

"Mm-hm. So are you gonna work at the record store or not?"

"Who's asking?

"Me."

"Yeah, sure," I say, unsure of what happened to his threat of keeping his distance for a decade, but I'm trying here. "Betty's not always here, so I'd rather not sit alone. Reason to escape...my head."

"Sounds good."

Click.

"What, no goodbye?"

The phone doesn't answer. Will must still want penance from me. Won't let me off his grudge ledge that easily.

When I was a teen and through my twenties and most likely till my early thirties, I'd envision numerous ways to beat someone after an annoying phone call. Rotary or touch-tone didn't matter. The clunky table-top phone was the way to smash a face. Hit the lame-wad with the handle or the base (the base being heavier back then). Could hook your paw into the cradle of that kind of phone. A perfect weapon. In the 90's, they became brittle. All plastic. Whacking a face with the rubber, bendy antenna of the cordless phones could be fun but cause minor injury. My aggression and fantasy to phone-strike lowered somewhere before I hit thirty-five (before cordless). Maybe because of a natural lowering of testosterone?

"Button, you asleep?"

She doesn't answer. Zonked out on the couch. Dead as the phone.

I'm sinking into the night and couch. My day's end. All of it—the quicksand. Only, this grainy muck isn't the legendary, adventure-movie version where you can't crawl out, where the hero, villain, sidekick, or peon stands there and lowers into the water ground without moving for fear of sinking more quickly. No way Jose. That's fucked fiction. You can swim your way out of quicksand. It's difficult, and you have to move faster than it's moving in on you, but it's possible. And that's me. With gumption. Not frantically struggling, but pushing through the grime with grit. Get-up-and-go. Gallons of that fuel still in me.

"I'm the motha fuckin' G," I say, startling Betty awake.

"God! What now?!"

CHAPTER 8

Damn it all to hell. I fell asleep on the couch. 6 a.m. Awake to no one. Betty's out walk-jogging.

Yawn. Scratch my balls. Debate on stretching before finding Betty. Catch up to her and scare her, maybe? She takes that trail through that patch of woods behind the supermarket. Spook her during a hot flash?

That was a trip, when we argued over whether or not men have hot flashes. They do. I've had them. I wouldn't admit it at the time, but I was rooting for men having the problem. Kept the personal evidence and what I'd heard about men's estrogen outside the conversation. She became loud. Felt invalidated as a woman who has different troubles than men. But I feel *I* was dismissed as one who could relate. Like women feeling sexualized and objectified on magazines. Next, will be average Joes feeling inferior and misrepresented by the celebrities who started pumping iron at fifty-years old for superhero roles, making people like me wonder why there wasn't that option back when I was that age. Proves it's getting just as bad for us men. Aw, Jesus to Hell, I'm not going through that debate again. Especially not on my own, in the quiet of my head. To hell with that. And when *was* that argument? Months ago?

I suppose I'm stewing. Sitting here with the rising sun, pouting at its support, keeping out the thoughts of guilt whenever I envision one of those nurses, even though I'm not looking to act on it (them). It's a different kind of contemplation compared to something like premeditated murder.

"Let's stretch, you bastard," I tell myself.

I do. Following my own advice. The demand.

As you get older, you learn a bee sting isn't the worst of it—the day, the predator battles, the anguish of summer. *Go ahead and stick me with your pointy black and yellow ass. I can take it.* What you can't take so lightly is when you have an inability to open your backyard umbrella. Less than twenty pounds, but the angle and the tender tendon in the crook of your arm, the one you pulled during softball practice at the ripe age of ten, has returned like a beastly-bitching mother. You've become unable. Someone who's developed a no-way-no-how. Any knowhow taking a hike and definitively settling down in your past.

That's what's a bummer. That's what I'm not going to succumb to. Wallow in my past like a beaten donkey? That's not me. Make life about my current vitamins (D and E) and probiotics, brain memory meds (that I don't take faithfully), fish oil (good for everything but a sensitive stomach), and the occasional iron supplement (and all the others for the decrepit)? That's not me either. I've taken something for blood pressure, and now I don't. Betty has had her calcium supplements and other stuff. But that's not all we are as a people. As old(er) people.

While lacing up—rare coaching being the only reason I'm caught alive in these bright sneakers—I watch a Hollywood Squares rerun. The original run. Been waiting for it to begin, aware of the time it airs, because I had such a good time watching an episode in the waiting room at the hospital. Wrote down the day and time and put a reminder on my TV as soon as I entered the door. A truly old man move, but to hell with it. I really enjoyed myself waiting, watching, and most importantly forgetting I was in a doctor's office. The program took me back to a time before its original airdate, when I used to dream of being a host. As a career. For years, that was my plan. I'd say, for most of my childhood, I pictured myself laughing with the contestants, holding one of those skinny microphones. Maybe it'd get me out of my shell. Maybe I would've been more than awkwardly mean when I opened my mouth. I was more than a "pretty face" and a "hard body," two descriptions I would never be caught saying out loud. Not till recently, over the past three or four years, have I ever felt safe to say words like those. Because a guy shouldn't say he's feeling judged by his looks. But I've gone over that.

Bet your ass I had some brains in school. Bet your ass I still do. Got the same thinker, don't I? I might get malicious, probably because my words don't sound as good as yours, but that doesn't mean I can't figure out something faster than you. That doesn't mean I can't beat your face in. That doesn't mean I wouldn't have humped your foxy lady behind your back to prove what a wise smart ass can do.

Those game show hosts? You *know* those guys were balling those showgirls.

But, no. My ambitions and interactions and connections wouldn't lead me to chasing tail and drinking like a fish, would they? I'd somehow, by whatever it is that spins the world 'round, instead be led to being a car salesman. My entire life, apart from working at a warehouse and in hardware and doing some odd plumbing and odd carpentry jobs, I sold hundreds of thousands of dollars (millions?) in automobiles.

I'm not ashamed of that. Fuck you if you think I should be. That's not my point.

I stand. My hip denies me the run before I get started.

As slow as humanly possible, without any shaking, I finger my laces and undo the knots. I remove each shoe with pain partying at my hip joint and slam the sneakers on the ground as if they were caked in field mud. I punch the wood floor of our dining room. One time. POW!

"You're not going to beat me," I say to the body that's momentarily not mine. I want to palm thump the hip, but

I breathe in the humidity, come close to destination Pass Out, and safely get off the jerky train ride, bracing myself against the door jam.

"What's going on with me?"

Betty or some other clunkhead would answer, "You're getting old," or something stale and flaky.

Only, that's not it. Not the only part to this metamorphosis. I'm finally too big for my britches. Expanding the idea of geriatrics. The blood flowing all over. Maybe warming up. Maybe for the kill.

I smile. Again, the idea of murder giving me something terribly exciting.

"You've got to be kidding," I say to the picture window, slowly making my way toward the clear partition to be certain of what I see: that jogger skipping along with my Butt.

"You just made the list, dipshit," I whisper to the glass.

In my head: "Who the fuck are you?"

Or: "She's old enough to be your grandma!"

Or: "Hit on somebody your own size. Your own *age*!"

I clench through pain, a crazed version of sciatica, to slip back on my unlaced shoes and come out of the house. Betty's breathing heavily as if she were riding the jogger, he lying back and watching her squeeze her tits in a grand finale.

She smiles and waves me over to join the conversation.

"This the guy you were talking about?" she asks, stretching skin to show a cartoon set of beaming teeth.

The jogger lifts his eyebrows, eyes on a weight bench–struggling. I used to bench three hundred. Knees acted up, so I was smart, protected myself, and sat my rear on a stationary bike. You can still work your whole body without the pressure on the lower back. My spine is hell and part of the reason I've shrunk from 6' 4" to 6 foot or so. Taller than this guy, though. (One of my lines to ready women for the sack was, "You're messing around with a six foot dick," until I once said, "I'm a six foot, four inch dick," and the woman ignored the first measurement and teased me for the second.)

"What are you two talking about?" I ask Betty, straining with my fifty-pound grin.

"How ya doin'?" he says.

I realize all three of us have picked questions as the safest rout to Social Street.

I want to ask how much he lifts, but I'm not in the right headspace to talk or, specifically, ask any more questions. I'm caught off guard, like the serial killer whose main weakness is his belief in his own perfectionism. (Recognition of a narcissist's selfishness is a protective factor for unsuspecting, defenseless victims all over the world. Narcissism is also a trait for murder suspects and may lead to being caught and, therefore, a reason not to kill an innocent person in the first place, which means I'm superior to the egomaniac murderer who's blindsided by the tactful detective who uses narcissism against you. A perfect, probable, non-narcissist killer, I am, if I *don't* murder.) "Hi," I say with no trace of hostility. Necessary or not, I want that hostility. Badly.

"Have a good day," he says. And gone.

He didn't ask for my name. I don't know his. Was that an introduction? Is it better not to be introduced to your worst nightmare? Because I'm going to be his.

I laugh, possibly pompously.

"Jesus, what now, Lance? You're giggling like a psychopath."

"Don't you ever laugh at your internal dialogue, Button?"

She doesn't answer. Cute as a button. I couldn't be turned off by her degrading conduct if I tried. Plus, I'm hard as metal, ready to bone.

"Did you jog with him?" I ask.

"Are you crazy?"

"Are you answering my question or changing the subject? Or are you on the same subject?"

"No, I didn't jog with him, you mental case. And why'd you just stand there like a nutjob? You're a mule deer in the headlights."

Why do that, Betty? Why throw in a memorable outing while insulting me?

Mule deer. The freakishly bald, tailless horse-animals we saw in Arizona. Right next to that animal crossing sign. I like those memories, too, you know. That was a good time, when we used mule in place of a curse word. Or saying, "Ass poop," every time a donkey crossing sign popped up.

But to reference that now? For what? A distraction? Is it a cry for help? Emotional help? Understanding? Or don't you want me to get personal anymore? Is that a sign it's over between us? Or *do* you want me to get emotionally close and open up? Create some new memories? Or would you rather I end it? Our marriage, our life together, my life, your life? Are you asking me, pleading with my sentimental side, to end what you have? Whatever you have going for you, or whatever you are in search of—you want me to end that for you, Betty? Cut it off? Or cut it out?

She looks at my shoes.

"Are you going out?" she asks my feet. "Jogging?"

"I was gonna surprise you. Hump you in the woods like the pope."

"So let's go. I haven't gone yet."

"I'm ready."

I hardly accomplish a slow fast-walk around the block. She continues ("finishes") without me.

CHAPTER 9

Before starting another day as a retiree working at a hip record store, I find myself scrambled. Peeling my egg-face from the bathroom mirror is more difficult than usual. Sometimes this is easy. Like sucking myself out from the quicksand sludge. Today, pulling away from the gripping slop is a goddamn nightmare. Me, I'm the nightmare.

The white hairs I meticulously pulled out once upon a time. Yanking until the tweezers became outnumbered and overbooked. The bright, coarse ones re-rooted forever in my head. Back then, my melon was getting patchy, too. I'd refuse to shave it bald. For the past fifteen to twenty years, however, there's zero contemplation. To shear or not to shear is no more, because I officially have a consistently, thinned-out cranium from front to back and side to side.

Take a look at my arms. The lack of tattoos. I hold no regret for the inkless skin, yet, there's a type of weakness that radiates from the glistening coating beneath my silver hairs. I look into my own eyeballs, right back at ya, back at me, and know I have no part in those groups of dumbasses. I'm talking about those downriver Michiganders (Taylor 'Tucky residents and Tennessee generations subconsciously rivaling the urban areas of Detroit for decades, procreating a false southern dialect, waiting to rise up).

My lack of Vietnam participation also taunts from the reflection. A biting rejection that sinks deeper than arm ink. And the one-leg-shorter-than-the-other peculiarity is more noticeable on the double me of today because of this bum hip.

But I won't be a bum with a bum hip. I won't let age define me. Besides, I'm not in the mood to be depressed this morning.

Soon after I arrive to work at the store, I find myself venting. Just for a sec. Starting with, "Fuck this shit," like that black gentleman who just stomped out of here. "The only thing this place is missing is white sheets and hoods," he said. I agree with him. Not about the place, necessarily, but the white guy he was talking to was a secret racist. Yes! A closet racist. Oh, Lord, yes! An implicit instigator. Hallelujah! That black man got me riled. Stirred my soul. I say, "That black cat was right." Standing here, bored, having nothing better to do than get lost in another's dream is the reason for my outburst.

Every time I see a black person speak out, standing up for him/herself, I still think of Martin Luther King, Jr. And I'm joining that stance right now, thinking, "Fuck these stupid people," the whole kit and caboodle for telling me my whole life that I make people feel uncomfortable or bad about themselves. I'll be helping, giving advice, accepting their complaints and justifying their significance, possibly identifying their bullshit as bullshit, and they'll turn around and stab me in the back, or turn around and walk away. Fuck those of the system. Here I am siding with a black man, thinking if anyone heard these thoughts, I'd somehow be blasted for using self-gratifying words.

Does this evasion usually happen as a result of people getting to know me? They think I'm going on about something and turning a situation into mine? Or do they believe I'm unsympathetic? Or that I don't know how to sympathize? Or that I choose not to? I'm asking no one, but I'm asking: what is it about me? And not having the answer, and having no one to ask, is pissing me off.

Once more, I'd like to say, "Fuck this shit," as free as the black guy did.

"You okay, Lance?" asks Jeffrey. Mid-fifties. Looks like the guy anyone would picture managing a vintage-vinyl store named "The Record Shop Vinyl Store" (a business name designed to mess with elitists and serious music folks). We carry rare thingamajigs along with the latest, popular albums. And Jeffrey's knowledgeable. Business savvy. Nice to talk to. But you wonder how much he truly enjoys wine vs. frozen TV dinners. Was he a nerd or a pothead as a kid? Did he ever marry? (I think he's married. I think he said. I wasn't listening.) But I'm asking if he's *really* married. You know what I mean? Does he talk to her about life or buy her flowers? Is his wife fat? Does she give blowjobs? Would he ever murder his wife, or a customer on the spot, in a fit of rage? Could he talk about these things openly if he had thought them? Does he see a shrink or get meds from a strung-out doctor? And where can I get me some? (Would he know that's a joke or, instead, hand over the number of his MD supplier? And how fast would Jeffrey rat out that mental health "professional?") Jeffrey adds, "You're kind of scowling."

"I'm told that." I rub my face like a mobster. "That I look sad when I think up good ideas."

"That's funny."

For weeks, I've been working the record store, and I think this is my first day of boredom. Contemplating racial slurs and reactions between customers. "World-weariness," Jeffrey once called it. "Your posture. The weight. It's sitting there on your shoulders, man."

"Thank you," I had replied.

Yesterday, I felt good about myself, my work here, my capabilities. I recommended Atomic Rooster, Rainbow, T-Rex, Free, Cry of Love (named after Hendrix's posthumously released album). For some good songs, Montrose and King's X. Of course, Small Faces, The Kinks, and Motown groups. "Funky Worm" by Ohio Players. *Fritz the*

Cat soundtrack. Foreigner's "Woman Oh Woman" or "At War with the World."

Some of the bands and artists I had to look around for, others jumped out at me as I walked the aisles. More albums have stayed in my head than I would've predicted. My favorite part of working here is learning about the new music. I say "local group," but some are three states away. Charlie Don't Shake, Books on Tape, James & the Rainbros. These bands aren't around anymore, but we have their albums on CD.

"Say Anything is an alternative group placed under a category of a category of a category of a genre, because they were doing something different," I tell these three young (early twenties) customers. "First album is the one worth your time." I feel alive, dependable, and indispensable until the one walks away. The other nods as if to say, "What's up?" for "Goodbye," and the last says, "Yeah, I'm familiar."

With all of it? All of the groups I mentioned?

"Are you looking for something different?"

"Yeah, boss, I don't know," he says, looking at the ceiling for another genre or a single spotlight with his name markered on its side. "I'm, like, thinking of some mixed sound in my head that probably doesn't exist. Pulpy Latin."

"Isn't that Tarantino?"

"Shit, you know Tino's work? That's wretched."

"Maybe you're a genius," I joke to crack his egg head, but he's so fucking dunced out on his own shitty life, he can't do anything but rearrange the part in his hair while modeling himself after himself in some helpless synagogue of lost brain cells.

I've also serial killed my cells up there with the booze but never from the mind-altering crap. Tried marijuana once. Thought it was for weak people. Drinking, however, is more like battery acid or hot sauce. We need liquids to keep on keepin' on, and I like the danger of inebriation.

Closing your mind and still going forward has always been a cooler idea than opening your mind's eye or talking about jazz.

"You know Curtis Mayfield?" I ask.

"He work here?"

I think somewhere along the way, way back when, I'd lost a taste for blood, to harm or kill, because the idea was popularized. More and more, over the years, the thick thirst has dwindled. The *In Cold Blood* killings was something. And in the late 70's, starting somewhere in the early 60's, probably with *Rosemary's Baby* and Zeppelin and Sabbath, the dark side of everything was everywhere. And everyone (kids, the new generation) became damned and flat-out devil worshipers. Around that time, death was in your face. The topic overkilled. A news-frenzy fad. Of little interest to me, to say the least.

Thinking of Satanic rituals and glancing at an album cover of the Dark Lord reminds me of my long conversations with that legitimate Satan lover. Worked with him at the car dealership for a year. Like Jeffrey, he was in his 50's. Older than me at the time. Set in his ways, yet, ahead of his time. And that was his point. Hail Satan, for his time to reign was afoot. *A-hoof.* Even though most of those beliefs died with the generation and my dark-souled friend. (I hope that didn't make me a friend of a friend, that other friend being the Devil, even though I found the worshiper and his purpose more interesting than the media-exploiting explosion back then.) After rumors and truths about Devil congregations, the world became depressed. Charred spirits offed themselves for a decade. Kid-celebrity addicts and overdoses bled into the 90's and the Seattle Sound. The heroin-burdened grunge people arrived on the scene to make black thoughts (and farmer flannels) snazzier than ever. I was in my early to mid-forties by then. None of it ceasing my search for good, hard rock from the heart. (Noting how alternative, three-chord hacks never supplied the proper amount of disparaging contentment for me.)

I'm pretty sure all those decades of pop culture moving toward creepy turned me away from wanting to look into my own gloomy side and stopped me from being a murderer. Not being a fad follower kept me from following my dream to end it all for all those followers.

"You like jazz?" I ask Wretched. "You could play a synth style of it over some Bach."

I'd love to show this guy my new list. Not of movies. My list of names. A collection of people and their essences. Maybe discuss how the names got on there. (Pen and paper, numb nuts.) The criteria for choice isn't detailed or explained on the sheet, but I'd enjoy divulging. He'd ask what the list represents, and I'd demand his name, and he'd give it, and I'd add it, mentally marking him as an arrogant guy unworthy of similar company on the list, let alone a list all his own. A self-absorbed monkey-man not worth his own existence. "What's that page with names all about?" he'd ask, and I'd say, "Wait and find out, sonny."

After writing "Wretched" on the list I've since stored in my corner of the register desk drawer (along with my car keys and wallet), I get a pump of pride. Because I've made it through the tormenting mud.

I've got the hang of being here and, more importantly, like the work. So quit bellyaching. I'm a salesman by trade. I'm good at it. Just today, I was asked if I'd like to take on more hours.

"What'd you say?" Ryan asks. He's one of the kid employees. Maybe not a teenager.

"I said, 'Sure,'" I say. "More hours won't screw with my social security check. So why not?"

"So Jeffrey wasn't lying? You really are over sixty-five?"

See?

"I guess I can see that," Ryan adds.

Fuck.

"I'm retired from my job as a car salesman," I say.

"Not from life."

"I hear that, dude."

The "dude" drools out of his mouth condescendingly, although I know it's not meant that way. It's in comradely fashion, yet, brings to mind the spit from a greaser and his milkshake straw, which doesn't fit the messy mouth-mistakes of this (his) decade.

None of this communication gap is Ryan's fault.

Ryan doesn't know what it's like to hear phrases change over the years. He's not aware that the aim of manipulating and shifting dialogue phrases is to weed out the old ones. He's never noticed his own smile twitch in the mirror, clueless that that's what your face does once it gets tired of making appearances in public. He has no idea how it feels to question your involvement or input in a conversation after you've done the math and realize you're thirty years older than everyone here, there, and everywhere within the past four days (and that you're keeping count).

At the end of the night, we staying open later than most others on weeknights (10 p.m.), I bag a customer's cardboard squares of music and say, "You'll appreciate those tires, I'm sure."

Ryan watches the customer as if looking for a reaction. I don't know why that would be, but I find that's exactly what Ryan's doing when he turns to me and says, "That's awesome." I don't understand. "Tires, dude." What? "Yeah, because...right? We're like tire salesmen." Tires? "We're all car salesmen. We don't retire. Ever. Ha! Retire!"

Ryan pats me on the back, so proud. And I'm the little boy who doesn't know the rules of the game or why they're cheering. Is it something I said? What'd I say? Tires? Cars? I think I may have misspoken.

After I convinced the guy our in-house pressed vinyl was a real part of the store, I confirmed the sale. For his benefit, I assured him he'd made the right decision and a wise purchase. Only, I didn't say LP, or vinyl, or album, or 7-inch, 10-inch, or 12-inch, or record, or even phonographic record. I said, "Tires."

And by next month, "tires" becomes our shop's slogan.

"Take 'em for a spin."

"Check the tread."

"Kick and needle those rubbers."

"Roll off the lot with a full set of four."

Today, a local band requests whitewalls. I'm congratulated; Jeffrey claims I've boosted sales. (Bullshit.)

In the meantime, I feel dumb. Like an old foggy fogey. I'd like to put the misunderstanding behind me, but reminders attack like flies all day.

A month and a minute after my slipup, Ryan says, "It's even a better term than 'wax,' right?"

I'm aware ageism exists at all stages and that I shouldn't be upset with ignorant, ambitious youngsters. Ryan, however, doesn't make my list for another reason. That is, I forget to write down his name.

CHAPTER 10

Lately, Betty's been turned off by my expressions. Face and words. I don't know if it's my age, but I'm sinking deeper in the quicksand of who I am. She can try pulling me out by disliking my approach all she wants. I, personally, think that plan stinks.

Five years, and I'm already feeling like I don't need Betty. Like I'm breaking apart from her. Sometimes, I wonder how I could get rid of her, thoughts she's also expressed towards me. During a tiff, she points and says for me to go. Sometimes, only sometimes, I wonder if one of us should pack up and leave.

The back cyst is an example of having to do something on my own that could have, and should have, involved Betty Button. She could've helped me examine the lump and told me not to poke at it. To stop being so rough with my body. She could've said to cool it. Relax. Stop trying so hard.

I used tweezers. Squeezed and ripped. Half the puss stayed in. My skin doesn't snap or seal like it used to, and I've created a scab. I'll admit, feeling lonely can be saddening and cause us to be rash, but there's no excuse. I shouldn't have had to do all that by myself.

When away from the mirror, I reached back to touch the booboo on my right shoulder and said, "You dummy," switched hands, and reached to the other side (staring at the cyst's reflection for too long had confused the hell out of me, making my left side my right). A quick moment of come-and-go inferiority. Like when you have trouble following an exercise, reminded how each year your coordination is going, going, until gone.

Can't do much of anything but hate yourself during times like those.

Now, back to facing the mirror—another day, another me, image there and ready for the taking—I say, "You don't have kids, and you don't regret that, and you've done a lot of..." and lose focus (and gain focus on losing something already lost). "That doesn't make any fucking sense," I say, knowing it does. No regret, though. I'm not experiencing *that*. Being old can simply be a lot to deal with. "Being older," I correct. "Older than I was," I say which, out loud, is a no-shit statement. What else can anyone be at any given point in time other than older than what one once was?

I look deep into my own eyes. One's larger than the other. My face is crooked, half droopy. My nose seems bent to one side, too. All these feature flaws seem to enhance over the years. I don't care about my dark eye circles or the hair-color loss anymore. The bright, coarse face-and-head stubble somehow makes me look dangerously younger. A prickly fickle pickle prick.

And that's no joke, when women bitch and moan about men looking better as they age. They're correct. We're more distinguished. A woman grows out her white hair and looks like a damned witch.

But those perspectives and trends tend to change over time. Weight, eye placement, outfits. Low posture on a woman is now sexy. Fat women are sexy. Tattooed women are sexy. Unnaturally-dyed hair is a turn on. Glasses, crossed-eyed, crippled, baggy clothes, short-cropped hair, shaved heads, pissed-off faces, smoking, facial piercings, body piercings, nuns, real freckly fire heads, non-Americans, big eyebrows, thin eyebrows—well, I'll be damned, I think even the wrinkles and long gray hair is sexy. I'll take it all. (Not the white hairs, though. Something about them screams banshee. But hold on a sec. An Irish banshee in a white cloak over white skin could also be fuckable. Maybe the best lay I'd ever have.)

I smile and catch the reflection of that devil sneer I can't help and say, "Not uncontrollable frizzy hair or mustaches."

No, I don't like that. Nor the dominant types.

Taking another gander at the honker in the middle of my face, I hear the dentist's voice talking about my jaw opening, how it opens in stages and how it's popping because it goes crooked before coming straight down as it's supposed to.

I had a ball in his lobby, for there sat this erotic Polish woman.

At the time, I was a little horny and upset with Betty.

Speaking bluntly, I asked the Pole her age after small-talk introductions, she and I being the only ones in the waiting room besides the single lurking fish in the tank and the TV's game show host from fifty years earlier.

"Sixty-two," she answered, no problem.

"Sixty-two?" I repeated with genuine surprise. "I wouldn't have pegged you for older than forty-five. And *good* for forty-five."

"No, sir. Sixty-two."

"How about me?"

"How about you? Jeez Louise, you come on hard."

"That's exactly what I do."

She missed that and said, "I'd guess you're from the same era."

See?

"No more than...sixty-nine," she said. "Seventy!"

Fuck.

"Sixty-nine is the age I wed my wife," I said. "My first wife."

"Married at sixty-nine?"

"The magic number."

"Remarried? Second marriage?"

"Nope," I said.

"Part of what gives away your age isn't you. It's our generation."

"What does that mean?"

"A guy or gal in their eighties, today, is usually sweet. Cute."

"That's degrading."

"Maybe a little. My sister's of that time."

"Kinda condescending."

"Well, I think part of the reason they're seen as cute old folks is because they were a different breed. They have more class than our insensitive, hippie generation."

Her accent was polishing my groin. "I've always been a sucker for Polish accents," I think I said. "Ukrainian. Russian. Hungarian."

"They're not all the same."

"I suppose not, to you."

"How old's your wife?"

"You're quick."

"That's exactly me."

Maybe she did get me. Because I took this as a return flirt.

"She's sixty-nine, now. Same age I was when we wed. I knew her a few years before that." Oops, that was a lie. I remember lying. "That number keeps coming up, eh?"

"Which?" she asked. Did she want me to say it?

Younger people wouldn't believe this type of banter among my people is allowed and usually considered playful without first having to be dipped in politically-correct, comfort-zones-of-the-marginalized dog shit. Believe it or not, women wanted to be taught how to throw a bowling ball or swing a golf club. They played along; I know that much.

I was getting the nerve to ask her her opinion on butt sex when my name was called. And she said, "Next time, Lance," because she now knew me for her own little list. *I'll put you on mine, too, darling.*

And I did.

Alright. It's time I quit my mirror-mirror-on-the-wall

gazing and exit The Record Shop Vinyl Store bathroom and return to the conversation.

"Mirror in the bathroom!" Ryan sings, the coincidence disturbing as hell. "Bueller, Bueller."

Jeffrey shakes his head. "Ryan wouldn't be quiet until I put it on."

I realize the song, the mirror reference, is playing overhead. I'm tired of hearing *Bueller* movie lines. They were better when they weren't nationwide catch phrases. I've witnessed other sayings become a part of our life, too. Bogey lines. Willie Nelson lyrics. Funny TV commercials. And I get what's going on. We're more connected through computers and phones and are supposed to enjoy the world-wide community or whatever the fuck. I just don't receive enjoyment from Internet fads.

Minutes later, The Stooges' "We Will Fall" is never ending overhead, and we're talking about crazies who kill musicians and celebrities, starting with John vs. Chapman then Tupac vs. B.I.G. and Andy Warhol vs. women and Marvin Gaye vs. Father before we get to Liberace vs. ...

"His lover, right?" says Jeffrey.

"I don't know," Ryan says, thinking this is a contribution.

"I don't think so," I say, more to Jeffrey who'd remember the incident. "I think his lover was shot and Liberace had AIDS," I say to Ryan, hinting he needs some culture in his life. "How about Bob Crane?" Ryan's face is blank. "*Hogan's Heroes*." Blank. "Sex addict." Forget it.

"Sharon versus Family."

"Family?"

"Sharon?"

"Manson."

"Kurt versus Courtney."

"Hell, yeah."

"Phil versus wife."

"Spector or Hartman?"

"Tanya versus Nancy."

"Sam Cooke versus...uh..."

"Brandon versus Fate."

"Brandon?"

"Lee."

"Bruce was shot on set, too," Ryan says informatively and confidently.

"No, he wasn't," says Jeffrey. "That was a movie."

We're getting off track. I feel bad for Ryan's ignorance. I leave before we talk about JFK or Reagan or the Black Panthers, never getting into Jim Morrison, Marilyn, the King, Jimi, Janis, or all the rest versus, and losing to, drugs.

This could be the perfect time to offer my idea of a t-shirt that reads "Got Harvey Milk?" but swear, whether one takes it as a pun about Mr. Milk's sexual orientation or assassination (because it's both), the irony won't go over well and someone will consider the concept homophobic, hateful, and inconsiderate. Which is what makes the absurdity of the line funny. If it were an evil comment against him, it wouldn't be a joke. In poor taste or not.

So I keep the idea to myself and, instead, listen to the radio coming through the overhead speakers near the entrance. I watch the rain fiercely punch and poke the cement parking lot, it having no luck against the rows of shiny, slick car finishes and windshields.

Instantly, I regret my retreat, sick of the radio announcer going on about birthdates and death-dates. I don't need to hear the list of everyone who's passed on. All those I've grown up with—no personal relationship, mind you—croaking. Leaving us.

Shut the fuck up about it and get the hell out of here with that. Quit with the reports and talks about their legacies, will ya? Give some credit *before* their demise.

I leave the radio annoyance and rejoin the group, slightly guilty for turning my back on the rain and dead from above. The conversation, of course, has gotten to those who have weird hang-ups about control, possession, and inferiority. All those crazies who have killed musicians and celebrities.

Murderers rehearse before acting out their work. I wonder if writing books about true crime or fictional murder mysteries counts toward getting used to the idea until you one day cross the line and perform the part you've studied so well.

I don't want to be a pseudo murderer.

Remember those killers who wrote to the newspapers? And the fakers who followed?

I take out my movie list and underline key words.

It's a Mad, Mad, Mad, <u>Mad World</u>
Dr. <u>Strangelove</u> or: How I Learned to <u>Stop Worrying</u> and Love the Bomb
<u>The Good, the Bad and the Ugly</u>
They <u>Shoot</u> Horses, Don't They?
<u>The Last House</u> on the Left
The Little Girl Who Lives <u>Down the Lane</u>
<u>Assault</u> on Precinct 13
Everything You Always <u>Wanted</u> to Know about <u>Sex</u>* (*But Were <u>Afraid to Ask</u>)

When <u>a Stranger Calls</u>
Sorry, <u>Wrong Number</u>
Who's that <u>Knocking at</u> My <u>Door</u>?
<u>Whatever Happened</u> to Baby Jane?
Who is Harry Kellerman and why is He <u>Saying Those Terrible Things about Me</u>?
<u>Who's Afraid</u> of Virginia Woolf?

The Texas Chain Saw <u>Massacre</u>
License to <u>Kill</u>
<u>Kiss</u> Me <u>Deadly</u>
<u>Night of the</u> Living <u>Dead</u>
<u>I Spit on Your Grave</u>

Will was right. Those underlined parts read like a poem—a very telling one.

I'm not so sure about the sexual implications or terrorizing that tends to pop off the page, but the paranoia of someone attacking me in my home and me retaliating with a vengeance seems likely. Or does it read that I'd attack a homeowner?

Where does the "I" in this subconscious poem of movie titles land?

My *other* list reads:

> **Jogger**
> **Registration Bitch (college)**
> **Dentist**
> **Will**
> **Will's nephew**
> **Paul (cousin)**
> **Bruce (retired)**
> **Nurse (fuckable)**
> **Elizabeth (Butt–Betty)**
> **Doctor (hip guy)**
> **Polish (woman)**
> **Wretched (???)**
> **Coach (mine)**

The descriptions in parentheses are goddamn disturbing. Obviously, for some of them, I must be somewhat worried about forgetting who is who. For sure, it makes for a detailed murder list. Someone could easily connect me to these people. I'm incriminating myself. Or is it an insurance of some kind? Just in case I drop the ball, someone else can take a shot. Like a treasure map, my notes used as the key.

In addition to needing an alibi, I must narrow down the type of person I'd kill. A woman? A man? A bad person? A politician? What race? How old? Over nineteen? Under ninety-nine?

Oh, shit. I have to scratch off the pedophile coach. Will

recently mentioned the creep's empty funeral. Apparently, he kicked the crud bucket some twenty years ago.

~~Coach (mine)~~

Truly, the list lacks focus. For instance, why aren't Jeffrey or Ryan on there?

I remember that each of the three question marks following Wretched had a different meaning. (The first questions if he should be on the list. The second is because I no longer remember a Wretched. The third asks why he's still on the list.) Am I keeping him on as a backup in case he returns to my life?

The list also denies the philosophy to embrace the world's offering of randomness. I wanted to be a cancer, not a placed and set landmine. The list can be a detonator of sorts, but shouldn't be a confirmation of someone's criteria, where the person qualifies for a deserving death. I suppose the person of choice has to mean something to me. I should know them. But again, why don't I add my work colleagues? Or Will? Or the dental assistant?

Who the hell is Wretched?

"What you got there?" asks Jeffrey.

Maybe prioritizing and securing an alibi is getting the order of murderous events all wrong, but it's currently of interest. I can't act until I have some setups.

"A movie list," I answer.

"I like movies," Jeffrey says, as if convincing me that the temperature of the coffee he's drinking is satisfactory. "But I always have a problem with the lack of realism in them. Things don't ever come together in the end the way they do in movies."

"I know what you're saying," says a strung-out, tree-hugging customer around my age. "Although I don't think you're right. I'll tell ya why."

"Let's hear it," says Jeffrey.

"Movies can be truth," says the sweet-breathed hippie. "The best way of seeing a truth. More than a big moment, even. Because it's whatever we pay attention to.

In a movie, they focus on certain details. In life, we focus on the bad and then feel unpleasantness represents life. If we were to connect one good thing to another, and recognize how it all came around full circle again at the end with a nice bow on top, then *that* would be our reality. You noticed it. That's what happened. Awareness of the good or bad makes the difference."

Jeffrey smiles, appreciative of this guy's wisdom, which I appreciate of Jeffrey. The hippie wants someone to listen, is all. "Are you saying it's basically a matter of perspective?" Jeffrey asks.

"Not perspective. What you pinpoint in that perspective."

There are cameras here. Evidence.

Outside of work, I don't interact with many people, so I have some anonymity going for me. Could I find a jogger who looks like me? Who is now limping like me?

What am I talking about? A cover-up? A weakling to match my weakness?

Cameras in the neighborhood, on neighbors' homes. I'm talking about getting caught, that's what. I need a nowheresville for old folks that's not an old folks' home.

Do hospitals have cameras? I think they do. But I could schedule a doctor's appointment, make myself known in the waiting room for a minute or two of the thirty, and slip out to a random exam room for some quick murdering. My alibi would exist somewhere between my appointment and the dead patient's schedule. But the cameras would catch me leaving. Eventually. Assuming someone somewhere would watch the video. Is the hospital bathroom a better spot? It should be fairly easy to lure a medical professional to the toilet. No matter what, I'll be seen entering and exiting the murder scene.

What about hotels? Do they have cameras in their hallways?

Do I have to escape to a mountainous region and attack a hiker?

CHAPTER 11

Although some people treat me as such, I'm not dead.

In public, I'm dismissed. Seen as someone with less money. Zero percent needs for gratification. Generally slower. Impervious to degrading interactions. An outsider. An alien who never understands the many changing facets of human life. As if the older (and oldest) generations walk around wondering what the fuck is happening to the sun when it sets.

Betty doesn't treat me this way. She knows I need more reminders than I did when I first met her. She knows my reaction time is sometimes delayed. But even at eighty-eight, don't you dare act like I don't know shit from shit and need an explanation as to why some shit's different from other shit. That's fourteen years from now, and my patience isn't going to be any better regarding that kind of uncalled-for treatment. Fuckers.

Betty's in a category separate from most. A unique bird feathered with history. I constantly think about her never having kids of her own. She babysat before I met her. As a job, as an adult, for thirty years. She and her best friend Roshell worked together those last few years before retirement. I seem to think about that part of her past without ever questioning her ability to nurture.

That Roshell, though. What a piece of work. A snob. A know-it-all. I don't understand how Betty can stand someone like that for so many years.

"Oh, yeah," I say, writing Roshell on my to-do list. Pretty pressing, it (she) is.

When I think of being the predator and attacking outdoors, rushing toward someone, I think of that Arizona trip and the trails where Betty read about stepping hard to scare off predators. "Walk with a heavy foot," she read. "Sound advice," I said. We smiled.

Something in my bowels (a lodged memory, a bad pepper) nudges me upstairs.

"I gotta take a shit," I say.

"What's that?" asks Betty.

The other day I was thinking: a marriage is like factory-pressed lumber. You need a year or two of weathering the wood before you really start using, appreciating, and reaping the benefits of it. You take care of the planks. Staining, painting. The amount of future care you'll put into the upkeep depends on how well you attended to it in the beginning. And, by this, you get an idea of how long that marriage (lumber) will last before needing to replace it, hopefully not having to do that.

"Hello?" she says.

"What?"

"You wrote something down and put it in your pocket."

"A reminder."

"Are you okay?"

That look of hers, of misery, is probably what compelled me to put Betty on the list in the first place. I don't want a reflection of inferiority and concern I don't carry for myself. That's the opposite of a funhouse mirror and leaves me gazing into a depressing-house looking glass.

"I don't like shitting at work," I say.

She chokes on her fresh green bean, laughing.

"I'd rather avoid it and relax at home," I continue, "but my prostate and all the conjoining parts down there ain't what they used to be. No longer working together as a team. I'm not in diapers, but for shit's sake!"

"Perfect dinner conversation."

"Remember when I tried those Kellogg's exercises for the sphincter?"

"I told you that's not what they're called. And we're still talking about your ass, by the way."

"Fine. I think I'm going golfing. For a change of scenery."

"Who are you going with?"

I haven't thought about that. Right in front of her, I

pull out my list, read over it, and say, "Will."

"Don't forget your appointment for your hip is this week."

"A check up?"

"A check up on what? No. The surgery."

"When? Am I going by myself?"

"No, stupid."

I imagine if I were saying those words to her, how the conversation could have gone. Is there something more demeaning in my tone? Because I'm, honestly, not bothered by her playful ridicule. "I'm driving you. You're going under."

"Under?"

"Yes."

"Underwear?"

"Don't be dumb."

"Australia?"

"Huh?"

"Like, Down Under?"

"Unless you don't want to. No, not Australia. Did you hear me? Unless you've changed your mind about going under. But that's scheduled with the anesthesiologist, so I wouldn't wait if you've changed your mind. You'd have to call them now. Haven't you told Jeffrey and work about taking time off? Before you and your golf clubs go twisting the night away?"

Maybe it's because I'd just finished defending my baby Betty Button internally that I'm outwardly sensitive and throw my fork at the wall less than six feet from me. Before I reacted, I experienced a nanosecond of worry about flinging the pasta sauce and the single noodle coming loose from the handle and getting lost and hardening beneath the stove. I did not, however, consider the utensil bouncing off the wall and hitting the side of Betty's head.

"Button!" I say, as if the words would shield her from the immediate past.

She slams her palms—or maybe fists—against the table like a gorilla and leaves.

I want to explain. I don't want the surgery. I'm pissed at the rabbits and their hole. I want to be stronger than someone who has to worry about divots. I was hoping you were on my side. I'm frustrated about justifying my existence at work. I hate shitting in public restrooms. I didn't want pasta because of the acidic effects tomatoes sometimes have on my tummy. I wanted to say "tummy" to you earlier, Betty, but never had the chance. I want to thank you for telling me to get out in the world more often. I want to share with you my idea to murder. I want to golf. I want less structure. I want more time. I deserve more and all of it.

"I'm sorry, I just wanted to golf this week."

Something KABOOMS in our bedroom. I can't imagine what it could've been. People use that phrase ("I can't imagine"), but I literally cannot mentally identify or visualize the object or area of the room where the sound occurred. And, again, I wonder if Betty has died. Passed out? Did a dresser suddenly tip over and flatten her?

To find out, to get a response, I say, "I've also been invited to go out and watch stand-up with the guys from work. Or with Will. I can't remember."

"What?!"

Alright. She's alive.

"Stand-up," I repeat. "Stand-up comedy."

I hear her grip the doorknob. She doesn't open the door. She's never done that. Nice restraint.

"You can do whatever you want. Go ahead. Go now."

"I'm sorry I threw the fork."

"Why?"

"Why?" I'm confused. "Why did I throw the fork, or why am I sorry?"

"I don't know. You tell me."

"Tell you what?"

Nothing.

"Why I'm going to stand-up?"

Nothing.

"Could you massage my hand before I go?" I ask, and she guffaws like a foreigner ashamed for the stupid American who's lost in the jungle. "Tonight, when draining the pasta, I had to adjust my grip–" She thrusts open the door, which I forgot is a possibility.

"I told you to use the colander."

"I called it a caldron earlier."

"I know. It's a colander."

"I know, Butt–Betty. That's what I'm trying to say. You care about me."

"Of course I do."

"I know you do."

"If I ask questions or correct what you're saying, it's out of love and concern."

"I get that. From a place of respect."

"Well, you sound stupid sometimes, so someone has to."

She smirks.

"And you massaging my hand..." I say. "I still need you in my life."

"Still?"

"I don't know."

"Do you have dementia?"

"No. Would I know if I did? But no. I don't have the signs. I'm, maybe, having some issues with retirement. My place in the world."

"Get more hours at the shop. Or ask for less."

"I asked for more. And now I'm having to have surgery."

Truly, I am relieved when I see the understanding in her eyes. The moment is magnificent. Why the fork was thrown, why I spoke like an imbecile or one suffering from and managing through brain malfunction, why I'd like a hand massage, why golfing (not now) might be good.

"Stand-up?" she asks.

"I don't know if I'm going to do that," I say, bashful. "And I didn't mean I wanted to golf this minute. Tee time would be in the morning."

"You should go if that's something you want to do. Before your surgery. If you're having a difficult time and have too much thinking going on upstairs."

"Where else would the thinking be?"

"In your pants, where your brain usually is."

"You know me."

And like that, I know what I need to do. Out loud, I say, "I'm going to call Will. After I clean the mess in the dining room and buy you an ice cream."

"I'll come with you."

And then there's what I truly and wholeheartedly need to do. Quietly, I take out my list.

Elizabeth (Butt—Betty)

CHAPTER 12

The first time I saw Aunt Julie in my reflected world was on my 50th birthday. No dad resemblance. No mom smile. Just my mirrored face wearing Aunt Julie's mask. Apart from having less sprouts on my scalp and more stubble all over my mug, I'm her spitting image.

She was an alright person. I didn't know her very well. Could probably say I don't know anything about her. Never asked. She and my mother weren't very close. They weren't estranged. Or maybe they were. That's how little I know.

I do know I'm older than she ever was. Good for me.

"Almost done, there, chief?" says a voice outside the door.

I open the door and present the closet-sized space to Impatient.

"Free smells for ya," I say, bumping his shoulder. With the little golf pencil, I write "Impatient (Golfer)" on my list.

Before joining Will on the course outside, I look over the list of candidates once more. "Jogger" at the top. My inspiration, you could say.

After seeing and speaking to him again this morning, I planned to place his name in parenthesis (now that I've learned it). I hesitated, trying to remember if Betty had already told me his name. And that hesitation brought about more hesitation. Which brings me to now, not positive on the name and zero parenthetical addition.

As he jogged off, I thought of the physical therapist who'd taught me about body scans back when I was in my forties. How to mentally measure my body movements and sensations. I'd first noticed favoring one side of my body during a set of pushups—an example of how we all compensate for hours and days on end. The therapist's advice helped me analyze my physicality. Slightly tilt in the opposite direction. Be sure not to buckle my knee or lean away from the tightness unless it's joint pain.

This morning's thoughts of aging, changing, and deteriorating continued, and the disdain and fed-upness I carried like pain came next. And after that, I thought of the different people whom I've known to die. Specifically, my buddy who had the pacemaker put in at fifty-two. All those Pacemakers. And all the others out there. The ones who wear the bingo visor hats or over-sized sunglasses. Those folks shoved into new wheelchairs for the first time for the rest of their lives ("Old-Mobilers"). Hunchbacks. White-haired backs. Nurse Homers and Nurse Homies.

I'm not sure what sort of title I'd get. I know I'm not the guy in denial who smacks his bicep or abs beneath a beer gut and says, "I still got it." That's something I don't have to say or prove. But I could see (hear) something inspiring. Old and tough. How about "Still Life"?

Before the jogger hopped away, he said, "I used to think running was a waste of time. I still do, kind of, because I'm just racing against it. Time. Losing, really."

I took a step closer to kick dirt over the horse shit he'd laid down and seal the generation gap between us, asking, "How long do you jog for?"

"I've been doing it for about five years," he exaggerated.

"No, how long is your run? How many minutes?"

"Oh, sorry. Um, about twenty-five minutes."

"I've got a tip."

"Love to hear it."

"I've learned over the years, a long time ago, actually,

when I was younger than you, that you have to at least get to thirty. Probably closer to forty-five minutes to really get something happening."

"Oh, I can't," he said, grinning like a toy doll. "I wouldn't be able to fit that kind of time in."

Bullshit.

"Maybe," he backpedaled, "I could add an evening run."

He wouldn't.

"Anything is what you make of it," I said, sounding more guru than ever. To water down the preachiness, I got down to earth and added, "You watch the Olympics?"

"Are they on right now?"

"No. I don't know. But I'm saying, a gold winner at the Olympics isn't wasting his time during the meter dash or all those years that came before it. So what justifies his, or her, that *person's*, success? Getting on a Wheaties box?"

"I appreciate the advice, man," he said, oblivious to my own race against time and adapting, and jogged off. Conversation over, apparently.

I should have yelled out, "Raise those knees!" Instead, I scratched him off the list. Not sure why. Perhaps, because I gave some of myself to him. No, that sounds stupid. Both childish and grandpa-like.

From the white electric cart with our bags of clubs, Will yells out, "Ready, old man?!"

"This old man played knick knack paddywhack with your wife," I say. "Gave a bitch a boner!"

On the green of the third hole, I confirm I should cross off Will but can't remember if he was ever on the list. I check; he is. No Will kill.

The good news: I have a new person. A player. An arbitrary wanderer of the earth. A non-chosen victim. A golfer who may be obscene and pissing in the bushes but is, more notably, getting lost in the forest. Dropping into the low dips of these golf hills. Near me. Dick in his pants. Good.

I have a weapon. A club. My hip hasn't acted up once today. Maybe because of the swinging and twisting. Odd, but true. Doctors and science don't always have the best remedy. Like jogging through pain. That works. I meant to give this advice to our jogger this morn. Silly, forgetful me.

Again, I recall Betty's tip about walking hard when you're the prey. In this current scenario, stepping with a heavy foot won't scare off the predator (since that is I), and I won't ever lose the prey in the brush *because* of his (the golfer's) heavy-footed calamity. Funny, how prey can walk hard to scare off predators while predators stalk softly to surprise prey. The worst thing to do is startle a predator and force him to attack. I refuse to be startled. Yet, hearing a narrator document my prowling ramps up my heart rate, the bloody muscle gizmo thumping like a son of a bitch. Doing something so out of the ordinary and against social instincts is livening, on the cusp of a goddamn fatal heart attack.

In the trees, now. Closer proximity. Anyone who'd pass by and notice this man losing his cool over his lost ball would move on, because the behavior is usual and nonthreatening. Nothing to worry about. No danger lurks. Also, he isn't a woman lost in the moonlit woods. And I'm not a disturbed man in my prime. We're two older, fellow golfers. A couple of guys strolling on the course. And the question of us relieving ourselves in the bushes isn't there, because we're civilized and the landscaping is too nice.

I watch his face and search for signs of pompousness. Justifying the head strike? Finding the nerve?

Not only haven't I raised the weapon above my own head, I haven't even adjusted my grip. I haven't thought of the body being left at such a short distance—less than a football field—from my and Will's tee-off point. Is that bad for me? Am I at risk? Is the baseball cap enough of a disguise? (Completely out-of-character wear for me as was the brief Magnum P.I.-Miami Vice trend I followed for a year. Tropical button-up shirts in my mid-thirties. If I gave a shit, could be pretty embarrassing. At least I'm not in that getup right now. Gain a reputation as the most tacky, amateur killer on the loose.)

Am I legally insane or plain losing it if I don't give a damn about getting caught or the morals surrounding the violent act itself? Or am I something else? Something worse?

My ankle twists and my hip awakes from its nap.

The ball! I've stepped on his goddamn golf ball! He's getting away, and I can hardly walk. He'll be in sunshine any second now. I don't know why the act is necessary, and I don't want to overthink the warped motivation I've established for myself, but I have to begin my life of killing. I have to act fast. Impulsivity must define willpower.

The little ball in my fist. My hip worsening ever since I bent over.

I aim, wind up the pitch, and throw the yellow sphere as hard as possible at the back of his gray-haired head. I miss. He looks my way, seeming to know I'd been there the entire time, and says, "Thanks, buddy. I appreciate it." I instinctively, or domestically, smile and give two thumbs up like a mute groundskeeper.

CHAPTER 13

At the next green: "Are you keeping a personal score, Lance?"

"No," I say to Will, scratching onto my paper the name "Other Golfer" and then putting a line through it. "Just writing a reminder."

"I've got your score. Don't worry about it. I won't cheat you."

I'm thinking of my cousin Paul. How he cheated on his wife. The core to his pussying out (suicidal tendencies). I'm thinking of someone having an affair. Someone who I thought was having an affair. Someone who *was* having an affair. Who was that? There's betrayal in this memory. Sneaking out a window when I was a kid. Sneaking out to kill someone my mom was fucking behind Dad's back. I chickened out like Paul. Too cold of a night in my jammies. Bad blood, my family's got. Weak, thin blood running on empty. An extended family curse, apparently.

"Is your nephew going to come around the record store?" I ask Will.

"I don't know. Why?"

"I wouldn't mind apologizing in person."

"It might stir."

"Stir what?"

"Shit."

"Because he's on parole?"

"I don't know that he's on parole! Shut up about that, Lance!"

Will's drunker than I'd realized.

"You should tell what's-his-name, your nephew, to come by," I press.

He doesn't respond. He walks away to take his shot.

I enjoyed the hunt of the golfer. I may have to plan more intricately than I'd originally expected. Set a date. A place. (Still needing that alibi.) Leave no clues. Make no connections. Research nothing that will connect me to the soon-to-be-murdered.

"See that guy?" says Will. "I'm going to hit him with my golf ball."

"You're drunk."

"I'm nervous. My brother's coming to join us."

"Really? We're on hole four."

"He's probably an amazing golfer. He's probably shooting around everyone."

"Is he? An amazing golfer?"

"I don't know."

"I never met your brother."

"He's probably going to sneak up on us and read us our rights."

"Why?"

"He's a consultant for the police. A psychological consultant."

"Like a, uh...what's it called? Forensic...?"

"Forensic psychologist? Not really. He's similar to what used to be called a criminal profiler. He can tell you better than I can."

Will's playing off his knowledge. Or losing confidence in himself. I'm not sure.

"When's this happening?"

"I'm very serious when I say he'll most likely show unexpectedly. I'm gonna quit drinking and be ready for him at the next hole."

"He would've had to have passed us."

"Exactly. The sneaker fucker."

"*Sneaky* fucker," I correct.

"No. *Sneaker*. He wears those comfortable shoes, I swear, just to hold them over our head."

That's a confusing statement. As we cruise to the flat of the hill, I see an average-sized, average-looking man around my age in a pair of thick-soled shoes. I feel threatened by his knowledge, courage, and footwear.

"Bob!" Will says, swallowing for sobriety's sake. He almost runs into the guy. "This is Lance."

"Lance," says Bob. "Bob."

"Shootin' with us?" I ask, probably testing out Bob's friendliness.

Bob nods. Great. The silent type. And a gentlemanly fucker, stepping back, allowing us to shoot while making room for our clunky, electric cart.

"Did you see us?"

"I saw Lance," says Bob. "In the brush and trees with one of the members of the group ahead of you."

"That's right," I say. "I was out there in the woods. You are correct." Already, guilty as all hell, I put my hand in my pocket and rub my list. Happy it's there. Petting it. Protecting it. Wondering if I should crumple it or eat it. Human reactions, when in survival mode, are so goddamn weird.

"I was telling Lance about your job, but I was lousing it up."

"Let me hear your description," says Bob.

"Well," Will says, aligning his eyes and shot. "You're a consultant to the police, but you've been an over-analyzer your whole life. So..."

"You're intoxicated," Bob states.

"And you're annoying. Welcome." Will swings and the white dot hooks to the right and shrinks to a spec.

"My intention is to help," Bob states some more.

Will has gone from a little boy ready for scorn to a manly man prepared to take on a brother's threatening arrival to a stranger who lowers his eyes in search of a hole. Desperate to bury his head. Or stuff it into a vision tunnel for immediate, temporary blindness. That awkwardness where a human looks like a turtle without a shell.

I'm not going to avoid this menace to criminality. I'm going in.

"So," I say, "Bob," taking my stance as if I'm going to piss all over the tee at his toes. And he's looking right at my dick, legs, and club, knowing my spread-out is intentional. "What's that called? Profiling? Do you profile your brother?" I smile. I make a beautiful shot. I dip as I walk away because of my stupid hip.

"When's your surgery scheduled?"

Goddamn. Here we go. Fourteen more holes with Holmes.

"This week. Thanks for noticing."

"I would have suggested a surgeon and aided you in getting an early appointment if you hadn't already taken care of yourself."

"I'm fine, thank you."

Will looks at me and his face says, *See? He's already trying make you his bitch. It's a play. Don't feed into it. Don't take the treat or allow him to pet you. Bite his hand off at the wrist. And, Lance, be careful, because I'm 100% scared of my brother, and I have been ever since we were boys playing guns.*

Will says, "What?" mirroring my grin.

"Nothing."

Bob's already taken his shot. I didn't hear it. Is he that swift, or was I that distracted? My guard's up, isn't it?

"Yeah, Bob's been doing the career thing backwards. You didn't start working for the police until...when was it?"

Bob waits for Will to answer his own question. Remember or do the math. Will does neither. A brotherly power play.

"Fifteen years ago," Bob nods, eyes closed as if saying, "I concede," during a chess match but not giving in to checkmate or giving the satisfaction of saying, "I resign."

"What do you mean, backwards?" I ask Will, allowing either one to step in and clarify. Bob doesn't. He's scanning our bags and clubs. I swear to God, he's evaluating the fucking trees and sunlight like an Indian. A Native American. Or a landscape engineer. Will eventually continues, narrating the legendary life of a medieval movie hero with underlying derision.

"Bob here has kids who are grownup now. A wife, a nice house. Made a good living throughout his twenties, thirties, forties, and fifties. Retirement talks inspire the man to go back to school when he's sixty."

"Fifty-nine," Bob corrects, eyes surveying the course.

"People still mistake me for fifty-nine," I say. Silence. "Rarely, but it happens."

"I'd peg you as seventy-four," says Bob.

"Shit," says Will, crinkling his forehead at me without moving his eyebrows. Jealousy has caused Will to be habitually unimpressed and disappointed by his brother's constant accuracy.

"So, Will," I say. "Your nephew is..."

"No," says Will. "He's not Bob's kid."

"Which?" asks Bob.

Will ignores and continues like the envious little brother he will always be. "So Bob was able to jump right back into the college atmosphere as an older gentleman, having already done his time, completing his four years back whenever. Got his bachelors like a good little boy. Bob, what was your major?" Bob doesn't answer. "Silence-ism? No, it was psychology, but what did you end up doing with it?" No answer. That's expected and how they've communicated all their lives. Probably in the same bedroom for eighteen years. "He gets his Ph.D. Already had a résumé in crime and stuff like that before he went back at sixty years old."

Will's such an asshole, saying "sixty" on purpose. Winking at me.

"Résumé in crime?" I ask. I try another way: "What's that mean?"

Will waits. Bob slowly walks away toward our struck and waiting balls. For some reason, the departure isn't rude but inviting. Maybe humbling? We both begin to follow Mystery Man.

"Fuck him," Will says to me, quietly. "He was arrested for something stupid when a kid and that got him in with the local police. Volunteer positions. He'd always had a thing with the department, schmoozing, and is now...whatever the hell."

"An investigator?"

"No. But sort of. Part of a criminal investigating analysis team." Again, Will's acting the fool. A habit when talking about brother Bob. "He went to the academy for half a year or so," he continues, also a habit. "You have to to get that job."

"At sixty?"

"There was a physical fitness thing, too. He's seventy-four."

"Physical agility test," I hear Bob mumble like a super ventriloquist.

"Which I'm not sure he took," Will whispers. "But there's no age cap in Michigan."

"So he's *my* age," I say. "Exactly. How he knew. Why he guessed seventy-four." I'm relieved.

"Part of why, yeah. He's also fucking good at his job. He looks younger, though, doesn't he?"

This time, *I* don't answer. When we're closer to Bob, I say, "Impressive, you being able to switch career paths at a later date." I think I'm trying to be funny, but where's the joke?

"Like I said," says Will, "he's always been nosing in on people's business. He just wasn't getting paid for it."

"Lots of serial killers in Michigan?"

"Everyone has a psyche," says Bob. "My frontline work is elsewhere."

I look to Will, not completely understanding Bob's meaning. Will says, "I could have done that thing they do in the movies, where they mock the person's answer as they say it: 'Everyone has a psyche.' Because I knew he'd fuckin' say it. Bobby loves giving that answer, because he knows no one's gonna know what he's talking about. Look at his face. You can tell by the way he's not smiling." Is Bob my arch nemesis? "He works in a jail, and he goes where the crazies are. But only one county, right? Not Michigan anymore. I don't think. They grandfathered in a grandfather. He's visiting. Right, Bob?"

I want to gloat, to bend Bob's antenna ears in my direction, as I say to Will, "I told you about the college practically kicking my ass out."

"The hospital?"

"No." I didn't want Bob to know that. "Never mind."

Have I always been a recluse murderer and gone unrecognized for my ambition? I don't think that makes sense. My skillset isn't in killing. Not that I know of. My heart, though, has always swished in my chest whenever I've thought of taking someone's life. Not out of anger. Not out of necessity. Out of having the willpower to do so. Having the ability to do it when so many others won't or wouldn't dream of such a crime. It's a choice and an action that also just so happens to be a crime.

In elementary school, my temper toward bigger kids wasn't rooted in defiance or opposition. I just had a short fuse and wasn't afraid of their size. A troubled young lad. Mostly during kindergarten. High school, my anger got bigger than the kids and the best of me. On and off the football field. Random, unrelated memories spinning like ornaments.

I'm thinking of villains, those doomed to seek out a life of crime and/or murder. Somewhere in there, in that theory or witnessing other's let go of their inhibitions, I felt an elevation or an alleviation. To be free. To be noticed as is. Not to cower. To do the very opposite of what was expected of you. And I never did that. I was never free. I'm not.

To Will, for Bob, I say, "Remember when I faked my name?"

"No."

"When I first met you."

"I don't remember that."

Yeah, Bob, I'm showing off. I'm revealing some got-away-with-it details about myself. Because I did get away with some things.

"I did that for years."

"I guess," says Will, bored.

I'm figuring I'm thrilled to meet Bob. Excited to stalk the hunter, my opposite. I think there's some envy melting through me since this guy has training and was able to go through college as a senior citizen. Jesus, that shows arrogance, doesn't it? He could have waited a year to start college and had some of his class costs covered by the government (something I learned when visiting the campus) but instead paid for his first year at fifty-nine. What a prick.

I won't say I've met my match, because I know I'm not a brainiac, but this is someone who can test me. I can see if I've really got what it takes to kill. And I've been known to hold my own alongside the smart ones. Above the dummies.

I also know I'm in training mode, aware of my status— a rookie killer. So don't you worry about that, Lance.

For shits and giggles, I'll wait till we get to the next tee, pull out my checklist, and jot down *Bob*. Stand shoulder to shoulder with the wannabe detective.

"Lance," says Will, shaking his head.

"What?"

"You're giggling."

CHAPTER 14

I'd like to perfect the game. Know how to handle a golf ball. I won't have this hope or inspiration later, but right now, under the dome sky and sun, I feel alive. The golf course truly can be a form of meditation. A getaway. An out-in-the-open hideaway. I smile non-creepily (I hope).

Fidgeting with my golf ball, trying to control it with my club, having no idea how, I realize I'm not one with the ball and unable to master the roll or bounce of the thing, of its energy. I also don't know how to properly swing. A new wrist cramp is catching up to the intensity of my hip pain. I'm very un-monk-like and becoming pissed off, to tell you the truth. This Titleist won't do a fucking thing I tell it. Entitledist is more like it. Fuck meditation.

"Lance," says Bob, "I was curious about your hip and interaction with the doctor."

"He didn't ask me to turn my head and cough, if you're looking for details," I say, proving my comfort with strangers.

Bob smiles. We walk. Between long pauses and what seems like a deliberate period of introspection (a branch of meditation?), he says, "In my experience, and the experience of others in a position similar to yours, patients are often informed of the lack of strength and mass of their leg muscles and coordination; however, some doctors—not all, mind you—fail to mention the length of the leg. Walking at our age, and managing a steady pace, is not a matter of hand-eye coordination. Or foot-eye coordination, if I may. Your legs are your longest limbs and technically take longer to receive signals from, or give signals to, your brain than, say, a move of the neck. Knowing the terrain is important."

"Get the hell out of here, Bobby," Will says with more hostility than earlier, having it to here with his brother, drying up for the past five holes. "You ain't ever been an M.D."

Bob closes his eyes and nods, accepting the shutdown from Will.

"I didn't mean to intrude," he says to me.

"No problem," I say. "I'll probably intrude on you later."

No smile. Not anything.

I can't put my finger on why, but I'm aware of Will dumbing down his words, and in a half-assed way to boot. Some people naturally say, "You ain't never," as part of their vernacular, whereas Will used the slang for emphasis but kept proper grammar to avoid a double negative: "You ain't *ever*." More specifically, I'd say Will's avoiding his brother's negativity and psychological ridicule. To me, Bob's entire lecture was odd, as if he'd edited out words like "because" and "that" before speaking. How natural did it sound to Will? Again, I wonder, what it was like growing up with these two.

"Who's keeping score?" Bob asks me, ready to tell me his number, checking to see if I have, or Will has, the scorecard. Bobby boy wants me to answer. He wants to see my list with his name etched at the bottom. There's no way he could have seen what I wrote when I did, but I bet there was something funky about how I folded the paper or where my eyes looked after I pocketed the thing.

"Fuck you," says Will.

Bob understands Will's meaning: *I've recorded your score. Back off!*

Do they have one of those unspoken sibling languages? Is Will as observant as his brother? He must be, because Bob does that nod with the closed eyes again, trusting his brother is keeping an accurate count.

Already, Bob's nodding bothers me. It's a tell, for sure. He deserves to be on my list for that alone. Dumbass bobblehead.

"You know, Lance, the worst thing I've ever done..."

Bob stops talking.

Was that a question? Does he need undivided attention?

Screw this guy. I'm not asking.

Will swings. Nice shot.

And that's when I realize Bob was pausing out of courtesy. For silence.

"The worst thing I've ever done," Bob re-begins, "is diagnose my wife. I'm correct in my diagnosis, but I've been making up for it ever since I verbalized my observation."

Will says, "That's stupid of you. That you'd do that." He looks to me. "He's told me this before."

"I was thinking of my conversation with her this morning."

Nothing else. That's it. Bob must stop talking like that all the time. You think it's a beginning, but he's wrapped up a life of pain by sharing a remembered conversation with us. He hasn't shared the conversation itself, but the occurrence. The complication it once held, holds, and will continue to hold.

"That stinks," I say. If there's a worse thing I've done out there, Bob's dilemma beats it. Briefly, my conscience is cleared.

Will says, "Why do those hospital questionnaires ask about homicidal thoughts? Isn't it true you can have a mental breakdown along with thoughts of hurting or killing someone and not be a psycho or serial killer?"

Bob, of course, doesn't have to answer. And he doesn't.

"Hey, Bobby," says Will, obviously tired of his brother's calm presence. "There's an open mic comedy show at the clubhouse. We should go. Yes?"

If he closes his eyes and nods again, I swear to Christ...

Thumbs up? Coming from Bob, I think that was worse.

"I'm game to kill more time," I say.

Bob looks directly into my eyes and says, "I'm game, too."

> ~~Jogger~~
> **Registration Bitch (college)**
> **Dentist**
> ~~Will~~
> **Will's nephew**
> **Paul (cousin)**
> **Bruce (retired)**
> **Nurse (fuckable)**
> ~~Elizabeth (Butt-Betty)~~
> **Doctor (hip guy)**
> **Polish (woman)**
> **Wretched (???)**
> ~~Coach (mine)~~
> **Roshell**
> **Impatient (Golfer)**
> ~~Other Golfer~~
> **Bob**

My last interaction with Bob was like a scene transition, and I've been getting my bearings ever since. Avoiding him. Currently, fixated on the previous bottom-list member, "Other Golfer."

Sure, I went ahead and wrote down the fellow sportsman I attempted to attack in the woods and then crossed him off. But why did I put his name down in the first place?

Specifically, in this case, I'm trying to recall my justification for keeping track. It's my first real fail; I know. So, a reminder to do better?

I smirk at what reads as "Polish Woman" and wonder

if I'll later believe it to say "polish woman." Replacing a proper noun with a verb. Some broad I plan to rub down. Not that that's anything besides a wild fantasy. Murdering her is more tempting than actually following through with what sexual temptation brings.

"Is that the movie list again?" asks Will, breathing into my ear like a homo unaware of a hetero's personal space.

I flip the sheet over. "I'm writing some jokes."

"Are you going to go up? You can, man. It's open mic. Get on stage. Front and center." He gets close and whispers in my ear, "Whip it out."

"Why do you do that gay horse shit?"

"I don't think a horse's manure is any different if he's gay. And, Lance, if I'd known you were gay, I wouldn't have teased," and then moves his hips weirdly while wagging his finger at the empty, crystal clear glass in his hand. Reminding me not to drink hard liquor?

"Are we meeting your nephew there at the comedy club, or are we waiting for him here?" I ask, irritated as all hell.

"You lookin' for a date?"

"Fuck off." I say, unable to shake off a smirk. "Besides, I don't even know his name."

"It's *here*, for the hundredth time. The nineteenth hole. The clubhouse. The Golf Club's Club. That's the open mic place. One in the same."

"I got it, I got it. The nineteenth hole. You can shut up now."

"You're upset because I'm drinking and you're not allowed."

Through teeth, what I want to be a smile, I close it out with, "You sound like such a queer when you drink," and damn it feels weak.

Will is a mindfucker, isn't he? Just like his brother. I also think he's playacting. Not sure he's had a hard drink since hole three or four. I think those were two club sodas he downed.

"You should get a scooter for that hip," Will says, smacking me on the ass inches from the pain, and sits back down. I don't move so to gain the upper hand. Don't react. Don't respond.

Getting an old-person, grocery-shopping scooter? No. A moped scooter? Now, that may be an idea. Give me something new to do around the neighborhood. Could be helpful during my escape from the murder scene. Because nobody would rationally tootle around on the slowest version of a mini bike after a murder. No one would suspect such mad behavior.

Is murder rational? Am I really going to commit the deed in my own neighborhood?

"What if you got a moped?" the idea also dawning on Will. "I don't think you have to register them or get a plate if you keep it in the neighborhood," he adds.

"Where's Bob?"

"Getting wings. Or in the shitter."

"You mean the Sand Trap?" I'm critically referring to the titled driftwood above the restrooms. I hate pun places like this. I would never have thought the record store qualified had I not found out "The Record Shop Vinyl Store" is some flip-flopped, cutesy bullshit (apparently switching the places of "shop" and "store" makes their store name rarer than others). So what the hell am I talking about? It qualifies way up its own ass. (Their second sign reads: "Keeping Records and Storing Them for Over 30 Years.") The place has always been a site for saps. Anyone who comes into the store smugly smirking at one of those two signs is a goddamn loser.

I turn the list over to add my fellow employees Jeffrey and Ryan, because I'm suddenly and highly annoyed by the store's new new-wave, trendy, cockamamie existence.

"Bob!" says Will. "Lance was looking for you!"

Bob, stonefaced, comes over and joins me at the bar. I've still got the little golf pencil in my hand when I flip the list facedown. Far too delayed. I form an unidentifiable expression, trying to think up a joke on the spot, because Bob's going to ask what I'm writing. I distract, thinking of magicians and misdirection, and say, "Diagnosing your woman. No good, eh?"

Bob's taken aback as if suddenly encountering a mirror. He doesn't appreciate the challenge, take offense, nor seem confused. He knows he's been caught off guard and redirected and is checking himself and the situation. I've used his own interrogation tactic to trip him up, and it worked. He's somehow managing to turn shame into a moment of self-reflection. What a fucking lunatic.

"Well," he gathers, "some believe receiving the right diagnosis, or offering the right diagnosis, is the end. Good or bad, the label may appear to be everything. Like that sign above the restrooms."

Come on. Was he listening to me earlier? No, I don't think I mentioned the Sand Trap restroom sign to Will. Not when Bob was around. No, I did. When we'd first arrived, I made a vague comment. Said, "One of *these* places," rolling my eyes. Along those lines. No way, this asshole picked up my exact pet peeve from that. It's merely a coincidence, me contemplating over signs and puns. The fuckface is trying to strong arm me.

"Funny," he says about the sign. "Thankfully, not literal, given that we are able to leave the stall."

"No shit," I say, pun unintended. Now, I'm the asshole. Hell, that's another fucking pun. Use it? "A bunch of assholes in there, anyway," I say, eyeing the bathroom. I laugh. Naturally, I think.

He looks to my list. Smiles.

"You're right," I say, understanding his nudge to write down the joke. And I do. How'd he know I was planning to eventually write a few jokes? Did he just control my actions?

"Plus," he says, "we see ourselves and others from one angle, looking out. There is no reflection of our personal outward viewing and..." a long pause, "...no way for another to know what we're seeing or thinking." Is he still talking about his wife and diagnosing? "We see people as doers, caregivers, lazy, monsters," he goes on. "We may be wrong. We may be right." He stops talking. I'm half listening, writing a few more joke possibilities. "Or there may be no right or wrong. We're interacting the best way we know how."

"Lazy monsters?" I ask.

"As individuals, we may have interpersonal identity changes. Our values are the same while our interactions have changed. According to others' growth."

"Is that how you profile?" I'm just saying words that I've tried out before. With him.

"I don't use base rate-information–general profiling– to claim accuracy."

"Bob doesn't guess," Will translates. I didn't know he was part of the conversation. I'm not sure that I am. I'm sure Bob's full of knowledge and great ideas, but I'm not terribly interested nor fully listening.

I see Will's nephew enter. He's a clone of the man I struck. He's the same man, but somehow different from how I was remembering him. (Which means what, exactly?)

He's heavier. Fleshier. He's also an offspring of the point-at-you-when-arriving guy. Will rises to greet him. I quickly flip my joke sheet to the kill-list side and place the nephew's name in parentheses immediately after Will says, "Wesley!"

Will's nephew (Wesley)

Kind of a feminine name. Probably why Will doesn't use it.

"Is your whole family full of W's?" I ask.

"What?" says Will.

Bob looks to my paper, enquiring with his gaze. He never asks if I'm writing out an inventory of some kind. I could say it's a bucket list and not be lying.

Will hijacks the paranoia and is the new lead judge awaiting my plea, standing at Wesley's side. I put my arms up and say, "Guilty," to Wesley, to break the ice, to be the bigger man, to be funny. "Wesley? I'm sober tonight, alright? No elbows."

And, like that, I've accidentally exposed myself. Bob knows another side of me. Many sides. A guilty man. A drunkard. A jerk with lethal elbows.

Will's waiting for me to say more. Probably, "I," and "am," and closing with...

"Sorry," says Wesley. "I was a punk when we first met."

"But you didn't deserve him clocking you in the jaw," says Will.

"I've been on parole."

How long ago? Currently? Are you dangerous and now pretend to be a good boy until someone goes too far? Are you reborn? A Reborn Christian? Is this an excuse as to why you didn't defend yourself when we met? Why Will is defending you now? Why you won't scrap tonight?

I shake Wesley's hand, which is gentlemanly. I'm happy with my performance. I'm clear on my meaning. I accept. He accepts. No more words are necessary. Time moves on. So do us men.

Bob, though, he's watching like a buzzing bug with a stinger. If he was a grinner, he'd display those whites right now. A big fat fucking smile before a mission.

"I'm going up," I say.

"Going up where?" asks Will, expecting me to reciprocate Wesley's apology, as if I shouldn't speak about anything until I do so.

"The stage," says Wesley, defending me, taking sides, already creating a bond between us. "Right?" In my head, I've crossed out his name. That easy. I'm not out for vengeance. I could cross off others, too, in that case. I'll have to revisit the list with this philosophy in mind.

"Uncle Bob," Wesley says, greeting his creepy, probing

relative with a blow-off, single-hand wave that's something between a baby bye-bye and a high-five, yet, more direct and authoritative. Something like a crossing guard. I'd forgotten Bob and Wesley are related and that they must have interacted during the holidays. Wesley's for sure heard stories about these two uncle brothers. I think I like Wesley. Writing down his name now seems hasty. (I'd erase Betty from the list if I could. She was always more a placeholder anyway.) I still want to know whose Wesley's parents are. Will must have a sister or another brother.

After a few horrible attempts at raunchy jokes to set the tone and rid the place of the prudish members of the club, the guy (the MC) refers to his sign-up sheet. "Put your hands together, everybody, for our first single-name comic: Lance."

At my age, physical reactions versus body breakdowns (a definitive inability to function easily) can be hard to pinpoint. Right now, however, I know what's happening. I'm shitting in my pants. Not literally, but close to it. I can hear my heart and have to convince myself it's not in attack mode.

The single step leading to the mini, foldout stage seems higher than it should be. My thigh seems unable to lift the weight of its own leg, apart and in addition to the hip malfunctioning. Closer to the man with the microphone, I suddenly understand shellshock. I don't know how to reach for that thing in his hand (the mic). I've momentarily lost my depth-of-field accuracy. I don't know how to shake a hand. I don't know how to smile or maneuver around the single human being before me. What do I do with the mic stand? I want to hug it, but it's like a giant pencil protruding from the ground. It won't hold my body weight that's suddenly increased, pushing down upon my kneecaps. I mumble, "This is like a giant pencil," to use humor as expected, only it isn't funny. That's wrong along with everything else my senses are offering me. Or I'm misjudging the preciseness of what my senses are bringing in. I think of how to say this, and the stand almost topples over. I want to have the power and choice to click on the thing (the microphone) in my hand, but it's already echoing my breathing. The mic shocks my lips. I mumble, "Oops," and say, "on second thought," because I apparently didn't know how close my mouth was to the piece of metal and plastic. I knock my tooth on it. More mumbling–sounds really–before I loudly slur, "I've got to be careful." I think my words were audible. "These chompers are the real deal." That's funny. I'm old and my teeth are the originals. "Rappers get gold teeth before they need to. But I'm an OG! Do you think they make gold dentures?" No one laughs. My voice is quieter than I thought it'd be. The single bitty speaker is out there at the edge of the stage, away from me, where I can barely hear myself. I'm messing with the angle of the microphone to my mouth hole. Shit, chompers chomp food and choppers are false teeth. Maybe I didn't enunciate. They'll think my teeth are false, and the joke wouldn't have made sense. Or is having to take care of my falsies funnier?

Each second of silence feels like a minute. The lights are dizzying. I wonder if sipping something strong would've made this easier or worse.

Here I go:

"I was gonna use the bathroom before I got up here, but I figured there's nothing but a bunch of assholes in there anyway." A laugh. The joke didn't come out as smoothly as I heard it in my head, but hey. Joke two: "Don't worry. If I were to piss up here, I'm wearing a diaper. A *man's* diaper." A hearty laugh from one guy. "I'm pretty sure my dentist is Italian. Dr. Fugazi's office? Have you heard of him? Well, fugazi means fake or something like that. One thing's for sure, I stopped getting gold fillings there." Another laugh. From the gut. A different guy. I thought this was supposed to be difficult. Are they pitying me because the MC (bartender) introduced me as a first-timer? Or is it because I'm an *old-*

timer? He said something about it being my first time. "The great thing about this place, my dentist, going there, is you get a root canal with a side of pasta." I'm on a roll. But time is going by too fast. On stage for under a minute, and I only have two jokes left. Does that mean my perception of time is going faster? Am I miscalculating? I clear my throat before my impression of a gurgly-voiced Italian: "'Hey-a, whatsa matta wit da spaghetti? I gotta meatball stuck in my burly mustache!' And that's his *wife* talkin'." Uh-oh. Some heads have turned. Some away. Some toward me. "You know, over there, the men cook while the women...uh..." I'm losing them. Don't they know I'm doing an act? The microphone and the PA system feeding me my voice forces me to explain myself. "Racism and stereotypes are not the same thing. Stereotypes can be correct." I sound bigoted. "It's not like I throw a sissy fit–" Oops. "A hissy fit when an actor from Britain, or Great Britain, or London, or whatever it calls itself over there, plays an American." I'm losing this battle. The silence is keeping me at it, somehow. "It's not like I'm talking about hating other races or killing them. I wouldn't need that kind of motivation," I say and laugh to give the signal that that was another joke. Bob's not smiling. I wave away the audience, a gesture I'm told is specific to my generation, and come down with the microphone. I snag the stand with some part of my body or clothing and tip it over. The bartender/MC saves a member in the front row from getting struck by the weapon and gently takes the mic from my grip.

"Give it up for Lance: racism's last chance."

A minute later, coming back to my senses as if out of a raging fire, I say, "Fuck them."

"I thought you were great," says Wesley.

"Didn't Stacy do this once?" Will asks Wesley.

"Mom? I think so. Chicago. She said they laughed their asses off. Just told family stories about you two."

3rd Sibling (Will's sister–Stacy)

I wrote her down for the hell of it. Maybe because she had her own bedroom while her brothers had to share. Fuck her and her luck.

"More jokes?" snoops Bob.

"Nope," I say, on edge, not giving a damn what he makes of my holy list.

Wesley says, "We need different types of demographics and representations of people in movies and books, but they don't need to push it so hard. Force them all down our throats at once. It's like a friggin' politically-correct orgy." He laughs at his own joke. "Maybe I should go up there."

Will says, "You sure about that? Look at Lance. He's still recovering. Hasn't even taken off that stupid baseball hat to wipe the sweat dripping down his wrinkles."

"I was funny."

"You were," says Bob.

My self-confidence, that kind that's a hunk of something in the center of your torso, is mussed. That wasn't as fun as I thought. Definitely different from karaoke.

"Hopefully, you won't die after that hate speech," Will says. Everyone's suddenly a jokester.

Bob asks me if I'm okay.

What the hell does that question ask of a person? Really.

CHAPTER 15

Since I'm not on a vengeance kick, and to prove how dignified murder can be, I enter the calm place in my head and review the list. See who else I can eliminate. That is, remove the names of those who don't deserve to die. (Trumping random selection from a list of selected people. Doubly ironic.)

> ~~Jogger~~
> **Registration Bitch (college)**
> **Dentist**
> ~~Will~~
> ~~Will's nephew (Wesley)~~
> **Paul (cousin)**
> **Bruce (retired)**
> **Nurse (fuckable)**
> ~~Elizabeth (Butt–Betty)~~
> **Doctor (hip guy)**
> **Polish (woman)**
> **Wretched (???)**
> ~~Coach (mine)~~
> **Roshell**
> **Impatient (Golfer)**
> ~~Other Golfer~~
> **Bob**
> **3rd Sibling (Will's sister–Stacy)**

My pencil (hand) shakes as it hovers, and I'm concerned. Having a hard time crossing off names should be the moral thing to do. Only, I can't tell if it's the "right" thing for *me*. This is troubling.

Right now, I want to kill Bruce. Badly. For no reason. Or unreasonably. Both being comforting motives. How great would it be to cross everyone off except Bruce? A retired man whose time is running out.

Or how about Bob? Focus on the good guy who has to go down. Him or me. Now or never. Use a highlighter. Or, better yet, leave the name all by itself, changing the list to a scrap of paper that reads: "Bob."

Looking at the names again, bouncing my eyes around as if the list were a hopscotch made by a three-year-old, I decide to revisit the college registrar bitch, the impatient golfer, the nurse, and the Polish woman. I want to confirm the no-kills.

I sit, overly aware of cushioning my squat-to-sit maneuver by pressing my forearm into the armrest of our couch. I don't always do this or always notice. I have many methods of settling before sitting or resting and don't necessarily celebrate those aspects about myself. I did a stand-up show today. I should be able to *sit* without assistance from anyone or anything, for God's sake. (That's kind of funny.)

Ever since I turned seventy, reviewing my capabilities has become an issue. Like how I haven't run anywhere in the past ten years. I golfed with a bum hip a couple hours ago, but fuck me on all fours. I can't have one day of spontaneity that involves high-energy, high-intensity, or high-performance without repercussions? That's all gone for me?

At this rate, I'll have to stretch before a murder.

On the other hand, I'm accustomed to body preparation. And going through with murder shouldn't be any different from every other move I make in life. I'd say I'm a rarity for having the forethought to avoid pulling a muscle before killing. The reason this hip shit's unfair. Stupid as all hell, seeing as I've been bending like a son of a bitch most of my adult life.

"How was golf?" asks Betty.

"Are you over there watching me pant?"

"No."

Great. She's walking away. Did I botch that moment?

"It was fine," I say. "Still angry that I went?"

"I was never angry. Concerned."

"About what?"

"Nothing, I guess. You were gone for a while."

"I can golf at my age."

"That's not what I meant either. Jesus, you're so crabby."

"I'm not. You're judging me."

"I'm not."

"You just said I'm crabby."

"You're right. Never mind, Lance. Rest."

"What the hell does that mean?"

"The word 'rest?' What do you think I mean?"

"That I have to nap like an infant."

"I didn't say that."

"That I'm stupid for golfing and doing stand-up. And I didn't drink, so I'm not so stupid."

"I never said you're stupid. I'm not thinking you're stupid. I didn't think you drank, either, because you don't seem like you did. But you're being just as mean as if you *had*."

"Judgment."

"I said, 'concerned.'"

"About what? Me or not me?"

"Why you've been getting so irritable. Closed off. It's not like you. I wonder if you should go to the doctor."

"I did."

"No. Got to the doctor to see about...I don't know. I don't know what I'm talking about."

"Then, *you* go see a doctor about your brain and dementia. I'll go buy a scooter."

"What? A scooter?"

"Yep."

"O-kay...And I don't necessarily think you have

dementia. But you may be unhappy with your life and...I don't know. What scooter?"

"Always the 'I don't know' with you."

"Well, I don't."

"Yeah, a scooter. S-C-O-O-T-E-R. To ride around. Why the hell not?"

She inhales patience and exhales freedom.

"What?" I say, sounding calmer. And I am, I notice.

"A scooter," she says, thinking. "Like that...that's an example. What I'm...your recent antics..."

"Antics?"

"A new job at a record store, golfing...in a *baseball cap*. Stand-up comedy..."

I inhale, too, trying to get some of that independence she just expelled. I'm not sensing any in my lungs. Hers only.

She says, "I appreciate you taking control of retirement and boredom. I'm really not judging you, Lance. I wonder, though, if there's something else going on with you that..."

"You don't know me that well."

It looks like that hurt. But she's still trying. For me. "I'm not wanting to bring up the past but...I don't...I can't figure out why you fought with Will's nephew."

"Wesley," I say, attempting to add on rational cordiality to the composure I could keep and hold on to if she'd let me. "Wesley was there today. Golfing. Watching me do stand-up. We're fine, now. I kind of like the guy."

"And now you're buddies with him? What is he, twenty-one?"

"Who gives a shit?"

"And the college disappointment. I know that was harsh."

"I'm gonna go back there."

"Where?"

"Yep."

"Okay," she says, cautiously and condescendingly.

"Why a scooter, though?"

"Antics. Yep. That's me."

"Go back where?"

"College! Why do you talk to me like I'm stupid or not making sense? The baseball hat?"

"I didn't know where you meant specifically. The same one? The same college? And I wasn't making fun of you. I've never seen you in a baseball cap. I didn't know you owned one."

"I didn't. I bought if for the sun."

"That makes sense. I'm sorry."

"Mm-hm."

"Are you going to ask for the dean...at the college? And why? To try to enroll again?"

"Hell no! I'm not being heard, Butt! And...aw, Christ!" I clench my fists like a teenager or toddler or convicted felon during a job interview. "I'm done calling you that."

"Fine."

Is she disappointed or relieved?

"It makes me feel," I begin, trying my best, "like you've got all these buttons I have to watch out for. Or that I'm not addressing *you*..."

"Do whatever. I'm not stopping you."

She walks away, probably to meddle with my head. I do some revising of the list before I get my shoes back on and zoom off, driving recklessly toward the college registration office (where I park in a professor's reserved space).

CHAPTER 16

"I'm sorry," I say to emulate this college kid's voice, in search of an adult and an overall approach. "There was another woman who was helping me. Before. A different woman. From this part of the campus. My wife was with me. She's better at this than I am. My wife."

"That's okay," says this person who doesn't seem to have a title or an official job but has somehow wandered from a classroom and qualified herself to offer advice and direction. "I'm sure I can help you."

We both discover that her advice and directions are ultimately wrong.

I return to the office (the counter) and carefully explain what I want to another person. Can't help. Sends me to another person/counter. I notice there are no cameras and am told this building is older than the others. The student probably thinks my age makes this useless information relevant. A little eerie, knowing there are bricks as flaky as I, I'll admit.

Next, I'm informed how this section of the building (this room) and all other information areas are soon closing. Odd to me, hours posted on a place that has people non-stop waddling, but fine.

Before leaving the Counters of Classroom Clowns, I develop a plan.

I have no intention to join their club or college or loans. Instead, I'll ask general questions while choosing a way to kill one of these office idiots. Before closing time, of course.

I ask two or three of my prepared questions and, before I know it, am in another chair. Waiting. Hating my hip. Feeling tired. Blink, and I've made it to an office with an older person who's younger than me (sixty, sixty-five). This one also seems to be figuring out the logistics of a possible registration for the first time in her life. But that's not my plan. Nor my "goal," to use her wording.

This is the time. This is *my* time. An opportunity to be the villain killer who strikes and stabs fear into the audience. Everyone running or hiding because the crazy serial murderer has a weapon. The audience believes the threat is because of the dangerous object the masked or shadowed person carries, only, their wrong. Their puny brains can't comprehend the deeper fear. Getting the upper hand is not explicitly linked to holding a knife, chainsaw, ax, or sharp object. What sets the murderer apart and gives him the power is his murderous ideals and his courage to challenge himself on how far he will go, especially with that strange, sharp object. It's more like the philosophy behind *Dr. Jekyll and Mr. Hyde*: it's a choice to be a monster. The genius doctor wants to revel in a no-guilt self. People, the innocent idiots of the planet, simply don't know how to respond to the unusual. And when those strange minutes take place, on a movie screen or not, the panic sets in, and the one who sets those death wheels and countdown clock-hands in motion is in full control. (I guess, in real life, I'm the murderer *and* the director. That's boss.)

Right here, right now, I have a leg up on this old bitch. Even if she beams and agrees I should be treated as elderly with loads of respect, she won't see me coming. She won't know my fist is mighty and that I can strangle her before any of the clown morons in the neighboring offices figure it out.

I'm so above this woman, this campus, this mindset of college and knowledge, that I leave her midsentence. Not only were we in the middle of pamphlet perusing and schmoozing, I was the one in the middle of a word. I stopped talking, walked out, and altered my list to those who are worthy of my time and calculations.

That registration bitch wasn't worth my time or the death service I could've provided.

~~**Registration Bitch[es] (college)**~~

And I add and immediately cross off:

~~**Idiotic Clown Students (college)**~~

Overall, I'd say it's been a good day. An easy, thoughtless final drive through the evening. I'm pleasantly pleased up until I get home to Betty calling me out on my writings. Not the list, the jokes I'm working on, or the movie titles; I have those in my pocket. She's holding another paper. It must be my work-in-progress.

"What the hell is this, Lance? *Man on a Mission*?"

Yep. That clinches it. The sun sinking, leaving us in a bizarrely half-lit living room. The title of my work said back to me. I get goose bumps. Does she get *I* am the man? *I* am on a mission.

"Memoirs, it says," she says. She's been crying.

"*Man on a Mission: Memoirs*. Mine. My memoirs."

"Uh-huh," she says with her eyes, confirming a shared understanding that hurts to admit.

"Betty, what you hold in your hand is not a mission statement or a manifesto but memoirs of a man on a mission. Think about the words."

If she read my *Man on a Mission: Memoirs*—red-ink-penned and corrected in a sort of bloody mess, centered down the middle and underlined all over with thick, ugly arrows to refer to earlier thoughts—that means she read how I'd like my pseudonym to be Scar Tissue. The entire piece reads like something I'd send to the newspapers as an announcement: my threats and plans and motives.

Delivering the finished memoirs was the initial plan. Give a few blatant clues about me and who they're dealing with. Send the original copy to local journalists. Go public. Get published.

"I didn't send it in," I say, more frivolous than defensive.

I wanted to be called out or noticed for my plan of attack, didn't I? Because I left it for you to find. By accident. By accident?

"I'm not the hero type," I can't help but say. "What else can I say?"

"What?"

"Hmm?"

"Lance, I don't understand. Why does it say that you want...Is it a joke?"

"I don't know."

"You don't know?"

"I don't know what to say."

"Did you write this?"

"Yes. But not as me. Not really."

"I feel dizzy, and sick, and I'm really confused."

"I've been thinking, lately, that I'm a bad person. Just as everyone has told me. My whole life."

"Lance, what is this?"

"It doesn't say I've done anything or want to do anything."

"To ki–" she stops herself before reaching the two L's.

"I'm the waste of the world. What's left of my time. No one wants me. And then, after living through that, I'll be gone."

"I don't understand."

"You're not listening."

"I don't understand. You want revenge on the world? Like a fucking teenager?"

"Butt, listen–"

I hear what I've said, how I've broken my rule to rid our home of the pet name "Butt," and look at the *Man on a Mission: Memoirs* in her fist. She has no right to judge what I've written, or force me to question my motives, or make this discovery out to be something more than it is. Because no one's read it but her. And I don't give a damn about her buttons or bullshit right now! I have my own buttons, for fuck's sake! I've had a rough day, taking the stage and working for laughter before a live audience and a psychological interrogator. After being so goddamned kind to Wesley and Will and, hell, Bob, and dealing with this grating, shitty hip, I'm emotionally and physically exhausted. I felt good about myself today, standing up for my beliefs. Even if the audience didn't get it (or me). If it weren't Betty Button but a brother going through my things, I'd be right to sock him in the nose.

I thump my hand against the couch. It makes no sound, because I missed the frame inside. I wanted to strike wood. Connect bone. I stomp away and feel a twinge in my leg, down from the hip joint, and I kick the fucking wall, because I want to destroy Button's bewildered expression. My action brings me back to the present. How I said "Butt" in place of "but" and how it had sexual connotation when it wasn't supposed to. This has happened before. All of a sudden, when enraged, the play name doesn't fit and I become inferior, like there's a sex symbol in the name I'm not recognizing or living up to, noticing the disconnection of my performance in bed, which isn't a problem, and would only seem the case if sitting with that Freud shrink. And any confusion is intensified. Am I looking for a nickname to hold onto, saying "Butt" like a lost kid, a young fuckup who's wandering the aisles of a giant store? I'm sure Freud would add that the grown man is a frightened, little dickhead constantly searching for a mommy-figure to rescue him from waywardness and impotency.

I've scared myself with just the right amount of wild, for Betty's sake (and safety), and manage to create physical distance between us. I make my way out the front door, glancing at the hole I put in the wall.

In the street, where the rain's starting to drop and smack the skin of my forever-thinning head, I'm proud I didn't hurt Betty. I don't wish to inflict pain on her— emotional or otherwise. And my outburst settles that.

I'll have to do something about this urge to ensure I won't ever attack Betty out of a desperation to take life, to fill my void. I must detach. Keep her safe. Satisfy my needs. Not to return until this is completed. That's the plan, even if it's the last thing I do.

She didn't mention the name Scar Tissue. Perhaps, the vagueness of the euphemism worked in my favor. But that might mean the name wouldn't strike home or scare the public.

The goal wasn't to create panic and massive fear, though, was it?

I wonder, did Betty already have an inkling about my tendencies? That reading minds thing she does. Does she know me better than I know myself, as they say? Because she's not chasing me out here. Maybe I'm playing out the inevitable for her.

Why didn't Betty say more? Why didn't she follow me? Maybe she's had enough of Lance's pants. She wanted me out, maybe.

You know what? I'll consider her indoor silence an agreement that it's time for me to skedaddle. And that's fine. I'll respect her wishes.

I stop walking; the sprinkles increase in size.

I wonder if Betty had already gone to the papers earlier today. "Let's figure this out," I say in the middle of the street, beneath the dark clouds and heavy showers, sky water saturating my clothes, face, and emotions. The amount of insight and understanding I have going through my head and body is intense. My outside actions, what probably look like the loss of physical sensations, are misrepresentative. Or am I overloaded with feelings and have *nothing* traveling through me? Have I blown a fuse?

A version of a panic attack. That's what this is.

The rain volume–sound and occupied space of wetness–has become trampling boots. I raise my voice over the noise to say, "Did you go to the papers, Betty? Did you go out of your way and ask them to publish the *Man on a Mission: Memoirs* for me?"

CHAPTER 17

You end up where you end up. Not underground, not in jail, but at Wesley's. A twenty-something-year-old businessman to whom I wouldn't be caught saying more than two words ten, fifteen years ago. I'm progressive, I guess.

"What's so funny?" my host asks.

"Nothing, Wes. Wesley. Do you have a preference?"

"Nah."

"I appreciate you doing this."

"I have the room. And now you do."

That was kind of smart. Why I don't mind talking to him. Because he isn't just an uptown, prissy boy, if at all. He's got something more. Something I admire in myself, I'm sure is what some psychoanalyzer would say. And I'd say, "No, psycho-anal-idolizer, self-admiration is not the only reason I appreciate Wesley. I'm not feeding into nor feeding myself my own ego or some psychobabble shit."

I also know there's more to my current outing because I visited Bruce before I ended up at Wesley's. Bruce was my first choice in seeking shelter, as in, someone who'd take me in for a drink even if I soaked the man's floorboards like a crazy hillbilly, modern-day cowboy barging in from heavy showers.

I had guessed and guessed right that Bruce had tired from retirement and was already bored. The truth was evident as soon as I sopped in. He kept returning to his piano. Playing it and pushing me to sing show tunes with him. And that's when Wes showed. My goddamn savior. They talked shop (about their record shop) for a sec and, before I knew it, Wesley swept me away like I was a princess trapped with a family of meanies.

Bruce was anything but unkind. He was hospitable. But being there with him wasn't my scene, is all.

I use Wesley's phone to call Betty and tell her I'm taking a break (not from us but from conversations) for a day or so. I explain that I'll get a hotel for night two if I feel the need to stay away longer. She appreciates Wesley for the stay-over. So do I. She mentions driving me to surgery this Friday. The topic almost becomes a moment for us to reconnect, so I end the phone call to put a cap on the confusion. We can talk after day two. I'm glad she agreed so easily.

"Can I use your bathroom?" I ask Wesley.

"Don't let me stop you."

He doesn't tell me where it is and disappears behind a corner of the house. Lots of corners here. Could open up the space to make it roomier.

Hello, Wetface, I think, imagining how Betty sees me when I'm like this: dripping, pouting, angry, saggy, real. I dry off with his towel. The thing appears newly hung.

Newly hung. I wink at myself before exiting. *You old dog.*

"I'm like a horny broad," I say for Wesley, who I'm pretty sure can't hear me. "Gettin' wet all night long." No laugh. So he can't hear me. Because he wouldn't have been able to resist at least giggling at that one.

I sit in the silence, sink in it, and that question repeats: *Did Betty go to the papers and ask them to publish my stuff for my sake?* It's like paranoia. Some type of instinctive insecurity.

That sulky mirror face. The eyes. I asked him: *Did Betty check to see if I already tried to get the papers to publish my work?*

I can imagine an investigative journalist being interested in my memoirs. The journalist would hear Betty's voice, the concern and panic in it. The pleading for a favor. The angle of an old man's manifesto. Headline:

"The Old Man's Manifesto Fiasco." Maybe the reporter is around Betty's age, attracted to her. Maybe he's younger and wants to try out an older woman. That seems less likely, but I'm trying to be fair in my thoughts, considering the possibilities, aware of the sexual desires of the real world, momentarily confused when deciphering and rearranging desires with faces and values.

Did Betty speak to Will? Earlier, when she first came across my papers? That's why Bob joined us on the course, isn't it? They, all of them, already knew. Some of them. Bruce for sure. Or maybe she hinted just enough to Will, for him to keep tabs on me. And Will, not knowing why, unaware of anything beyond my bits of crazy they've all been mentioning, asked Bob to come around and evaluate my sanity like a copper.

Many pieces seem to fit and are believable enough that I should stay aware. Or is the word "alert"?

I haven't been thinking clearly about who my enemies may be. Who else would know about my idea to kill?

I wonder if Betty tried to get the jogging guy to befriend me. No, that was too long ago, before I'd jotted down anything about Scar Tissue.

Was Wesley tipped off? No. I trust Wesley. Bizarre, but true. Why I'm staying here tonight. And the proof of Wesley's reciprocated trust for me lies in the bedtime story he's telling about his past. The tale's relaxing and distracts me from my world.

"And this was back when I'd return bottles," he's saying.

"You know," I say, stepping into the used skin of an old man before I can stop myself or deny my own actuality, "I remember Michigan being the first to get the bottle return laws going. I was probably around thirty."

"Oh," he says, genuinely interested. "I assumed it's always been that way."

"And being from Michigan, you probably didn't know there's less than a dozen states that do the bottle returns."

"Is it for environmental reasons?"

"Probably," I nod. "I think so. Hawaii got with the program when you were just a rug rat, I'm pretty sure. But, hold on a minute. No, stores used to want them returned because they were theirs. The ones they sold."

"It's still like that. Which doesn't make sense to me, because I thought stores were supposed to accept bottles from anywhere."

"I'm no expert. I just lived it. Can't remember all the details." I shrug. "I'd be a shitty history teacher."

Wesley shrugs, too.

"We used to litter a lot," I go on. "Crazy, when I think back at how many times I chucked food or wrappers or cans out the window of my car. It wasn't even a big deal."

"Now, someone does that with a can, a homeless person will be there to catch it."

"Or someone laid off."

"That's true, too."

"I'm pretty sure it's illegal to throw away cans. In Michigan. But people still do."

"That's kind of what I was saying."

"Go ahead," I say and, no exaggeration, snuggle into my pillow—straight from a jabbering geezer with boring memories to a little kid getting tucked in. I want to hear his tale.

"So, when I was returning bottles as a kid," he says, "I got this idea to buy my Mimi, my grandma, pop instead of beer. At first, it was to get her—who practically raised me—to stop drinking. She was a functioning alcoholic, my Mimi. Functioning quite well in the fuck-up category. As for taking life by the balls, she was squeamish. At best."

Normally, this style of talking would get on my nerves. But, just as before, I don't mind it when Wesley goes at his words in this way. Seriously, honestly, I think I'm coming around to maybe accepting people for who they are. As long as it doesn't drive me fucking insane.

"My plan," he continues, "was to get her to drink a pop. One single can. One less beer. A beer replacement, you know? Because beer was all she drank. Loved the taste

of it. Sitting outside or inside or anywhere with her cigarette, beer, and Whore. Whore was her unfixed cat. That
feline got around."

I laugh. "So instead of a man and his dog on the porch
with a guitar, your Mimi was out there with a horny pussy
named Whore." I laugh again. "She sounds like one of the
good ones."

"Mimi was cool. Not your average grandma. No
guitar, but she had a piano. She might've been a virtuoso."
He ponders over this missed attribute, giving a moment
of silence. A tear? "So, I was in charge of taking back the
bottles. One of my chores. She let me keep the ten cent
deposit for the pop. Because all this time, the beer-bottle
returns were off limits. She felt it was a bad omen or a
wrong kind of lesson if I took deposit money for those.
Plus, beer deposits went toward more beer, which I
couldn't buy. For Mimi, it was one trip. Return and put
the cash toward a case. Or maybe just one can."

"Another thing about Michigan—I'm pretty sure—
we're one of the only states that has ten cent deposits.
Others are five."

"I knew that."

"Keep going."

"So, quickly, the single pop added to more pops."

"Because she was an alcoholic."

"Exactly. She couldn't keep up with the replacement
pop. And having more pop in the fridge increased the
chances of her opening two of them and, you know,
allowing me to have the rest of the other pop before it
went flat. I wasn't allowed to drink pop unless we were at
a restaurant. I'd sneak one with dinner sometimes, too.
With tacos."

"You little shit."

"I wasn't a bad kid. Just testing the waters, you
know?"

"Sure," I agree. "You could have been worse. You
could've been smuggling beers to the garage instead."

"She would've noticed that. I think."

"Weaning granny off beer, eh?"

"Barely. But she *was* drinking something—I won't say healthier, but less unhealthy than beer. And it didn't take long for me to convince her to buy a case of pop. I had to show her the math of how it was cheaper than buying one can or bottle, which was easy, because it was true. She agreed, and I was now making a dollar twenty per case in bottle returns. Because the pop-return money was mine. She hadn't gone back on that."

"Was she drinking all those pops?"

"No, I had a spot in the garage where I stored them. Stacking high like my dollar bills."

"I knew it," I say, smacking my hand, rooting like a child. "It's always the garage. You *were* a sneaky shit."

"She knew I was putting the case of pop in the garage, because it wouldn't fit in the fridge. Because of the beer. Beer always in stock. And if the pop stayed in the garage for winter, they'd explode when frozen. So, she began drinking more of the pop. More taco nights."

"A good cause."

"A win-win. And when you factor in the sale days, double coupons, bargain days...I realized there was a pattern. And kept it to myself."

"You didn't tell Mimi about the price drop and pocketed the difference."

"Yep. Because what *was* the difference? This was my work, my walking, my plan, my looking out for Mimi. She never cared about the price of her beer. When she needed it, which was always, she'd buy it."

"Hey, you don't have to defend yourself to me," I say, eyeing Wesley's business shark teeth.

"The kicker came when I discovered the bulk sales. Stocked up, saved more, and never let her in on the difference and the money I was making on bottle returns."

"I got that," I say, possibly sounding frightened, thinking of asking him to leave the light on after his story.

"At this point, she felt obligated to drink pop. Open pop cans replaced open beer bottles. And she didn't want to dump out flat pop. Appealing to her emotions, in a way."

He stops abruptly. Is the cry after the anger spurt coming? Is rage about to happen? Are these legitimate twists on people's personal emotional coasters?

"When she was dying that last week in the hospital," he says, "I confessed. I showed her the money book of how much I was making back then."

I'm calling bullshit.

"It was more than the allowance she was paying me."

"She was still paying you allowance?" I ask. "Mimi Moneybags over here."

Wesley's face wipes away my grin. The same face I elbowed at the party. He's not looking at me, but there's a pain molding his features as angry or someone in agony. Is he proud? Regretful?

"Lance. This sounds made up, but on her death bed, before a coughing fit, she said she knew. All along. She knew what I'd been doing. And she thought it was great. We were both helping each other out. And what I was doing, probably for a period of, I don't know, two summers. It helped her justify when to pour out some of those beer bottles and cans."

End of story.

"When are you going to see Betty? It's Betty, right?"

"Yeah. Why?"

"I wonder if she's wishing for you to come back." I'm irritated or sad. I don't know. "You look tired, Lance. I'll talk to you tomorrow."

Just like a kid shocked by the turning of the last page, Mom or Dad skipping out and leaving the innocent, little guy in the dark...that's me.

"Wes, you have anything to do with the name of the record store?"

"Record Shop, Record Store. Vinyl this, Vinyl that. Hell no. That was Bruce."

"You're going to make some serious cash with that place, aren't you?"

"If the wheels keep on turnin'."

CHAPTER 18

"That's because you didn't listen," I tell the self-righteous customer. I lie and say I was present when it went down. "You asked for the 'all black guy.' Early rock. And Ryan here said Johnny Cash. Next time, double check what you're getting. Because Johnny Nash is *not* the same guy."

"I know that, now, buddy," he says. "That's why I'm returning it."

"But you also didn't listen to the album. Because that's a quality Nash album."

He smirks at me like a hitchhiker denied the long haul but invited for a good twenty miles. "Alright, man, that's probably true. Fuck me," he says, shakes his head, goes to the section marked CASH, walks to the register up front, and buys the correct album while keeping the other inside his armpit.

"See?" Ryan says to me, replacing his modern jive slang with my line, us both watching the man's low self-esteem shopping routine. "You can't take time off now."

"I am, Ryan," I say. "No going back. I came to tell you personally so you wouldn't be left with your dick in your hand and the schedule in the other."

"Jeffrey does the scheduling."

"Well, maybe your dicks in each other's hands, then."

"What?"

"I need to sort the rest of my life out. Tell Jeffrey that Wesley will be coming in to beef up the place, anyway."

"Who's' Wesley?"

I leave it at that and leave Ryan inside the store as I exit from some of the darkness, pulling myself toward light. Formulating a theory. Something about music fitting my time on Earth. That my life has been looking for B-sides. Day-to-day missed tunes (mostly rock). Not replaying the ones I know. Not searching for new music. Definitely not wearing out hits.

In the parking lot sun and air, I'm refreshed. I attribute this sensation and my theory-making and sucking in new life to Wesley opening up about his own shady past, telling me that humdinger of a tale before dreamland. Detailing how he discovered his strengths and used them for personal gain and accomplishments. I appreciated how he talked to me. Like a person and not an elderly elder. I was able to listen to his history. There didn't have to be an age hierarchy or any of that bullshit. That fact staying with me.

Or maybe I needed to get out of my home and head and step into a bright pit of unknown. All by myself. Out of a job. Out from retirement. Into my own existence without any attachments.

My suspicions of Betty going to the papers is shrinking. I should be able to let that minor period of mistrust go with both hands of the clock.

Bottom line: things look new today (at least, right now). I may be catching up to, or onto, a hopeful and preachy thought. Feeling revived. Anew, I guess.

Tonight, night two, I get a hotel room. A me-time repeat. Applying a different meaning to waking up. Part of this is due to drinking those dinky bottles in the fridge. I had to knock them down just to diminish the shock that hotels still offered mini parties.

And with the awareness and perky, wide eyes secure in my face sockets arrives suspicious characters. I notice one in the hall near my room, another at the bar downstairs. They look like perverts. I don't want to kill them for heroism, but I'd like to clear out and clean up what's around me. Whatever may or may not interact with my face, body, and movements. My lone, fresh night at the hotel spent cleansing. If I could wash away some of the shit in the world, why not? "I'd need a lethal sponge," I mutter and laugh. No one to judge my madman brain-heckles in the long hallways. Murder with a sponge? How about stuffing a guest's mouth with a washcloth?

Not as funny.

How great would that be, to off hotel guests in their sleep? No threat. No fight. Just end him/her/them. Room 218, 219, 220.

I giggle some, because how would I get duplicates for all those keys?

I'm also finding humor in the soft and squishy weapon choices (a fucking sponge?), especially since I've never thought of having a weapon in the first place. An absurd realization. Never thought of where or how to buy a weapon. What kind of killer would I be without one? That serial killer in the movie who's misinterpreted as dangerous because of the weapon, as opposed to having the will to kill and power to instill fear, nevertheless, needs a damn weapon. I'm not planning on adding up bodies past three, but a non-serial-killer killer is just as important as the next. His ability to follow suit is based on that weapon. Isn't it? I'm not sure I know what I'm talking about.

What about that fuck-o in the hotel bar ignoring that provocatively-dressed lady? Could I put him in a tight headlock and be satisfied before he'd ultimately stop breathing? Would I wrap a rope around his neck? Or use my fingers? How about knocking someone over the head with a bottle and then, what, maybe bashing their face into the concrete? That sounds stupid and immature. Run over someone? That seems removed, me watching from the bumper.

Remember, Lance, when you first jogged. Somewhere around the time you were refused to fight in Vietnam. A good ten years or so before that running book came out. (What was the title?) The new concept of running around parks – a universal homage to the hostages of the Munich Olympics Massacre, perhaps – had fit well into your sports days and playing in the yard with the local college kids of your own age. You'd dabble into feelings and thoughts of inferiority as the others left to study or picket. You'd finish the ballgame (whatever sport was revolving around whatever ball that week) and leave to fuck and/or fuck around. Breaking shit like mailboxes and windows. Slashing tires. You vandalized a couple dozen times on your own just to see what you could wreck and, let's be honest, get away with. Sort of fighting boys, sort of contest pissing. During that time of moseying around town, you had a couple nice rides. Hotrods for the hot pussy. The '65 Mustang: five years old and mint. The '69 Camaro Z/28 was mint and—what do you know?—that was also five years old by the time you got your fingers gripped around its steering wheel. Maybe that's why you get a boner for women five years your junior. The Chevy Nova: another '69 (not so mint). Drove that one through most of the 80's. Fucked a lot in it.

"What do you think about that, Betty Button?" I say to the hotel hall's cheap and peeling wall paint, feeling guilty immediately. Feeling bad for Betty. Like a brat forced to self-reflect. And I think I'm asking myself the question of what I think about my past.

Am I afraid of Betty leaving me? Is that why I still play with the idea of being a sexual, single-man?

The answer probably has to do with the number sixty-nine.

I smile. Back to enjoying my own company and humor, thank Christ. But I'm not just being funny. I recognize how the age of sixty-nine links Betty and me. My age when I met her. Her age now. Still not sure of the significance beyond the sexual position…

About four rooms down, a door opens and closes. Or

was the door already ajar? Were they listening to me? Watching? Didn't this happen when I first checked in?

I wish I had a hammer. A tool belt. Some fake repairman getup.

As a teenager, I used to pretend Peter, Paul, and Mary's song "If I Had a Hammer" was about murder in a church. We got a kick out of it. (*I* did.) Driving around with that song blasting like I had a screw loose. Later, in between rides, I'd jog without headphones. The movement would diminish a need to hurt the returning college boys and vets constantly punching my ego bag. Stomp the earth. Go somewhere. Wherever they weren't.

How I feel now, roaming these empty halls.

What the hell time is it? "After midnight, I think," I mutter in place of a cuss.

I step into an invisible incline and curse my hip (making sure to cuss), highly aware of my turtle walking. Worse than a turtle, because those old, bald reptiles look strong as Popeye, reverse flipper forearms pushing their hunky shells around. Envisioning the young-me, back when I car cruised, helps lift my spirits. I feel warm in the chest, picturing that version of me, no different from the guys in that movie with Ron Howard when he was a teen (drawing a blank on the name of the flick). I used to love ol' Ronny and Andy. And Fonzie, too. I enjoyed *Backdraft*. The only movie I can think of that Ron directed. Unless that was Rob Reiner. I used to enjoy Meathead alongside the Bunker family. Wasn't he in *Spinal Tap*? Did Ron have something to do with that movie?

I'm mixing up Ron and Rob's directorial credits, wandering through useless thoughts and halls with a useless body, falling apart and grasping onto crappy memories to make myself feel good, distracting myself from Button loneliness.

But I'm also allowing the change. Gearing up. Knowing my vessel is ready to take care of business. Part of the push is from paranoia (and the booze), but cutting people out of my life before cutting them and taking their lives is going to help organize my thoughts and get me feeling less at mercy and less mercy overall. I'm going to learn where I do and don't have control. Where I can and cannot follow through with my thoughts. Through actions. And Button somehow should be a part of that deducing.

Another hotel door closes. Or it was the door at the stairwell. No one would take the stairs at this hour. Is that an actual opinion of mine, or do I simply want to be left to my hall?

Find that strength from within. I *am* that strength. Find it and use it to kill a lingering sicko tonight.

How should I begin? Befriend someone? Ask them to have a drink? Get a call girl and snap her neck? Nah. Flimsy. Not worth the thoughts, even. The preplanning isn't me. It doesn't have my name written on it. I don't feel a connection to strategies like that. What's my stamp? My calling card? Why do I always go to empty sex and full-to-the-brim violence? That's an animalistic thing, isn't it?

Lobby has a nice wide-open space. No one watching. I don't think. They'd have to be sneaking and peeking behind one of these pillars.

"Sorry, bar's closed," says the bartender. Should I kill him?

"When does the pool close?" I ask him.

"Two hours ago."

I think I will kill him. I walk over to the bar, stumbling a bit.

"Sir, did you not hear me?"

"I heard you," I say, teetering on a stool's uneven legs.

"I'm closing up."

"Go ahead."

"I'm calling it a night. And I can't if you're in here. It'll get dark with no lights on."

"You've got that right."

He's about to say something smart but loses his macho stance. Gives up. Doesn't care. Been a long night for him.

"Alright then," he says and walks around the corner. The overhead lights die. Miniature brown lamps stay aglow between the windows and booths.

I'm going to use the stool to hit him in the back of the head. I pick it up, and my hip gives out.

"Oh, fuck." As I collapse.

"You all right," he asks, far too pleasantly. Far too urgently.

"Goddamn it."

And just like the western's pissed-off horse who's whipped by the overly-ambitious movie lead, I trot away. Cramp and crooked. Fast to slow, lost or dumb in the head. An obedient, bruised horse wearing a pair of useless fucking blinders. A useless and injured animal. Or a scared turtle. A joke of a snapping turtle. A beast headed toward nothing.

"Have a good night," he says.

What a fucking prick.

CHAPTER 19

Back home. Done with hotels and stayovers.

Going through our stack of bills. Old bills. Paid bills. The bursting, plastic accordion folder of paperwork that has spilled out of Betty's dresser and onto the floor like a dumped bag of leaves or a torso of intestines.

I hear a *sntt* before I see Betty at the bedroom doorway and the sound-making crab lady behind her, Roshell.

"Ladies," I say, keeping my eyes on the papers spread across the bed, my signal for them not to disrupt. At least, not while the annoying spectator is about. Can they tell that through my glasses?

"Lance, what are you doing?" Betty cautiously asks.

"Yeah, Lance," Roshell hooks on. "What's up in here?"

I so badly, bad-boy badly, want to ask how Betty can stand Roshell. She's the evil teacher from 3rd grade. How, as an adult, can one befriend a thing like that?

"I'm not really doing anything that needs to be justified, am I?" I look to Roshell and say, "Hello," my glare asking if I've given her permission to come into our home and speak directly to me.

"I'm going to go," Roshell says.

"Thank you, Roshell," Betty says. "I don't want you to feel..."

"Invasive?" Roshell asks.

"Is that what the kids are saying nowadays?" I say.

"*This* is invasive," she retorts. "I'll leave it to ya, Betty."

"How kind of you," I reply, flat as a pancake.

She leaves, and I respect Betty not turning to watch her friend exit. Neither of us offering Roshell any kind of goodbye.

"See ya," I call out, having the last word over my last word.

"Don't," Betty says.

"I'm sorry, Butty." Safe to take off my glasses and look at my wife with respect. "I'm sorry. About Roshell."

"Roshell?"

"Never mind her. I'm sorry. About the other night. And..." I look at the papers. I look at my list. Five seconds of noticing the names out in the open and, somehow, finding the moment pertinent to review them. Concentrating on the order. Reminding myself to draw an arrow from Roshell's name to the top of the list. I do that now.

What a demented degenerate I am, falling into an ill-timed or illness-timed distraction.

"Lance?"

I look at her face. She's concerned. Not about the list but about me and my wellbeing. My pausing. I mustn't stammer.

"I love you, Betty." I look to the papers. "And to make things easier, I'm getting rid of the extra, unnecessary paperwork they send with the bills. I've created a two-inch space in the drawer already."

"Great." She takes it all in for the first time. "You're throwing away the correct parts, right?"

"They're paid bills, but yes. We don't need to hold onto any of this these days. Statements and payments are all going digital. There's a lot of paper waste in this world. After doing this, I think I understand it better." I point at a stack. "That's garbage."

She sighs, but it's a welcoming. I can tell.

"I don't want you breaking or throwing things in the house," she says. "That has to be an agreement."

"The fork? That was uncalled for. Immature of me."

"Of a seventy-something-year-old man? Extremely."

Does she not know my exact age?

"It wasn't that serious of a fight," she says. "You were frustrated. The moment's gone." She's reviewing, convincing herself. "I'm glad you're back. Happy you're here. Of course I'm happy you're here."

"My house, but yes."

"Don't push it." And from friendly to serious: "You have to respect me, Lance."

"You're right."

"I don't think I need to say those words, to be honest."

"I agree."

"And Roshell can screw off," she says, sealing the pact.

"That's the ticket. So, online billing. Let's take care of all of our bills online. I've heard Roshell brag to you about it. She's an airhead, but maybe she's on to something. Maybe get rid of receiving mail altogether."

"I don't think that's possible."

"Junk mail. Get us off their lists."

"What about letters? Invitations from friends and family?"

"Do we get those?

"We do."

Ridding our private world of people is not so easy.

"Why did you leave?" she asks, softly. "It would have been better had you stayed. Because I think we need to talk, calmly, about what's going on with you."

"What's going on with me," I say, emphasizing *What's* in the form of a statement instead of questioning *going* or *on* or *with* or *me*. *With* could've been stressed but would've sounded hostile.

"I don't know," she says. "Like, what are you thinking lately?"

"What *am* I thinking?" I put my glasses back on, back to business. Am I coming off as rude? "I'm joking, Betty. I'm fine."

I, again, go over the different possible inflections: *What* am I thinking? What *am* I thinking? What am *I* thinking? What am I *thinking*? Luckily, I didn't put the emphasis on *I*. That would've made me sound unstable.

"You're sure you're okay?" she asks. "You don't want to talk about the other night or that..."

"The *Man on a Mission Statement*?"

"Your memoirs."

"Right. You didn't go to the papers with it, did you?"

She tears up quickly.

"Hey, hey," I say, sounding like a weak, young actor from a 90's sitcom. "It was a venting experiment. I got mad. Confused. I kicked a hole in the wall, which made me feel worse and reckless. I was trying to channel thoughts."

I was also scared that I'd hurt you or of the possibility that I was capable of such an action.

I pick up my kill list and hide it under some papers.

"Look," I say, standing and holding her shoulders like a first dance. "I'm going to put this junk in the recycle and...that doesn't make a lot of sense. Is it still junk?"

"Huh?" she sneezes because of the tears, snot, and dust. "What are you saying?"

"I think my brain is hungover from the comedy night."

"But you weren't drinking."

"That'd be a good excuse if I were, but no. I think that was the problem. I was too—what's the word? Lucid? I've been going in and out of feeling like a jokester. Got joke residue in my brain."

"Recycle being junk. Is that funny?"

"Thanks, Betty."

She smiles. Because the two of us really do enjoy throwing punches. Under normal circumstances, each of us take them well. Right now, we're like teenagers who never had the chance to teeny bop together. I think we both are aware of this feeling. I'd really like to slow dance right now.

I say, "I'll fix the hole in the wall, too."

"And the one in your head."

"Yes."

"Can we talk about that, though, another time? Soon?"

"The mission statement stuff? I'm tossing it. But sure."

"I'd like to...get to the bottom of it."

"Me, too."

Shit on me.

CHAPTER 20

To stay positive, I think of not having kids. That sounds like a backward way to sort your thoughts and emotions, but it's working right now for me, so fuck you.

Betty didn't have kids, and I feel bad about that. In a sympathetic way. And since I'm traveling that path with her, we're on the same journey. I believe that qualifies me as being empathetic. An upgrade.

Do I regret not bringing a junior Lance into this world? No. Could I wipe one or two humans off this planet? Sure. Can Betty take that path with me? I doubt it. But a smidgen of hope is better than a certainty of nothing. That's being hopeful for something, I guess.

The papers (bills, envelops, junk) are thinned. We have room for pointless mail filing for Betty and my future.

I next contemplate getting rid of our gardener. Because what do we need him for? He's one guy. Local. Slightly expensive. An unnecessary expense. An expendable person. We can mow and garden on our own, rabbit holes and hip injuries or not.

Put thoughts into action.

A phone call, and he takes it like a man. A whiny, passive-aggressive, lawn-care man, but a man all the same. Knowing when a job is forever finished.

Who else could we not rely on? Where else are people taking up space?

We, as a nation, have considered the gas-station attendant obsolete. Bank tellers replaced by the ATM.

Retail cashiers have been thinned. Many assembly-line people are gone. In the process, mail carriers have been compromised. In life, as time goes on, we don't need these people's services.

Could I truly get rid of our postal-service person? Open the front door and chomp? Swallow him whole?

Let me see that list.

> **Roshell**
> ~~**Jogger**~~
> ~~**Registration Bitch[es] (college)**~~
> ~~**Idiotic Clown Students (college)**~~
> **Dentist**
> ~~**Will**~~
> ~~**Will's nephew (Wesley)**~~
> **Paul (cousin)**
> **Bruce (retired)**
> **Nurse (fuckable)**
> ~~**Elizabeth (Butt–Betty)**~~
> **Doctor (hip guy)**
> **Polish (woman)**
> **Wretched (???)**
> ~~**Coach (mine)**~~
> **Impatient (Golfer)**
> ~~**Other Golfer**~~
> **Bob**
> **3rd Sibling (Will's sister–Stacy)**

Bruce was nice enough to let me into his home, and I wouldn't want to leave his piano with no one to serenade over the lid. So he should be out.

~~Bruce (retired)~~

I'd forgotten about Bob.

I remembered to bump up Roshell's name.

Will's sister? She's a target, isn't she? And no direct connection. (I'm still having trouble rationalizing how to randomize my first kill when reviewing chosen names from a check sheet.)

"Why do you want to speak with her?" Will asks me,

not really caring why.

"Her son's a pretty good guy."

"Wesley? You guys are butt buddies now?"

"Absolutely. We're renting gay porn and having cocktails tonight."

"Ha, ha!" Will's laughing, openmouthed, managing true "ha" sounds. At my joke? At homosexuals? At me and the situation? Wanting his sister's number? Should I get back on that stage and show that MC what I can do?

"When you golfing again, idiot?" I ask him.

"Did you enjoy yourself? You were pretty funny that night. And with no drinks? Maybe getting out like that is good for you?"

"I didn't ask for a playback or AA advice. I was just wondering."

"You're a dick. Yeah, I'd go again. Am I bringing Bob?"

"If you give me your sister's number."

"Do you have the hots for her? She's a female, you know."

"It's for Wesley."

"That doesn't make sense."

"It's none of your goddamn business."

"Fine."

And he coughs up the phone number like evidence.

There's that tingling again. A sensation. Would probably be easily identified and described in a kid book, but I can't figure it out. The shivers. Like a kid in a pool under overcast skies, the body jolting and ready to bolt. Because I'm making a deal to put myself in harm's way, around the block from a real possibility of getting jail-time. Because I've swung woods and irons with an old-man investigator and am now premeditating the murder of that very investigator's sister. Asking for the number outright. That's why the rush.

"Don't fuck her," Will orders.

"I wouldn't."

"It was a joke."

Not a minute later, through the bathroom door, I say to Betty, "The tub's drain cover is full of your hair."

"See how much you stress me out?"

"Look!"

She comes in and leans down, getting a whiff of my toilet surprise.

"Screw off," she says, plugging her nose, throwing a clean towel at me to lighten the load of quadruplets she was shoving into the closet. Still sitting, I block the entrance between my thighs before the cloth's corner dips into the toilet water. "I'd appreciate it if you didn't begin conversations with me while you're on the toilet. Thank you."

"They're the best kind. And I'm concerned. Surprised you have any hair left."

"Well, I'm shocked you have any of your asshole left. It's unbreathable in here."

"My shit don't stink."

"Right now it does. Holy crap." She coughs. "Never mind the holy. That's the devil's doing!" She exits, lively and full of blood today.

"I think I ate something not so good."

"Probably stress."

That's a real condition, isn't it? An upset stomach from worrying or too much hard, icky thinking.

"Close the door."

"Hold on," she begins. "Not to upset your tummy some more but—"

After a beat, I'm intrigued more by the cautionary silence than her unfinished sentence. "What?"

"I think we've got a flat."

Because I drove onto uncharted land. The alley in which I turned around. To get to Wesley's or the hotel. One or the other. Someone's trying to stop me from reaching out and strangling me a sister (Will's sister, that is). It's a common thought, but is someone or something truly out there blocking me from getting what I want?

"Because I'm trying to get ahead," I say. "That's why we've got a damn flat. A literal way to stop me from moving on with my life."

"Jesus, Lance. Don't be so pessimistic. You made some room in the dresser for papers, and now you've got a flat. They're not related."

"*We're* not related."

"That's true. By marriage, however, we are."

"However we are." She looks to me to see if I'm baiting her. Purposefully getting under her skin. I'm not. I don't think I am. "I'm playing around. I know we're married for good reasons."

"Okay."

Damn it. Damn this trust problem with which we're now tinkering. Inside, checking for bugs, kinks, and malfunctions in our five-year-long marriage.

"Okay?" I ask for confirmation.

"Okay."

"I'll limp this one out."

"Which means?"

"Hopefully, it's a slow leak, and I'll take it to the tire place up the road. It's less than a mile back. I'll walk it. Limp it."

"That's not a plan. I'll pick you up."

"When's my surgery?"

"Tomorrow."

"Then, there's no time to waste. This could be my last trip on foot."

"Not true."

"Last limping stretch, though."

"Maybe."

And on my straight and boring sidewalk trail back, after dropping off the car, I feel stubborn and dumb because the hike is too far. But I'm not going to rely on anyone. Not a phone call. Not a rescue mission from Betty or anyone from the tire joint.

There's a motorcycle shop across the street.

"Fuck it."

I've often lived by and preached the advice of never buying anything new. At least attempt to keep the old. Repair, if you can. Because the new part may befool you. And what about when you have to replace the old crap you've repaired? The buying or replacing never works out in your favor.

Only, in this case (convincing myself, trying to find space and time for that life-long theory), I know I'm not just purchasing a shiny, new moped. I am, but I'm not only doing that. I'm getting back at the flat tire and the overused and that which is scrapped. A comforting form of change or replacement within the boundaries of my principle. To hell with anyone who doesn't get that. It's an impulse revenge with room for failure.

The biggest motivation to cross the street and buy the mini-bike probably came from the eyes I felt on me during the walk. Not like I was being followed, but peepers judging an old man as mad or eccentric, all because of his lopsided jay-walking.

I had to make a decision fast. In hindsight, I could've bought a used scooter and stepped within the confines of my theory. Either way, I've made the purchase and am pulling up to the driveway on the two-wheeler.

"The cherry on top," I say to a confused Betty, holding onto sanity for the both of us, "no insurance needed." I rev the bike two times, a brat satisfied with getting into trouble, if only to be noticed. My purchase, my impulse, my way. No highway threat necessary.

CHAPTER 21

Yes, getting rid of people is hard. But, somehow, befriending and savoring them is proving just as difficult. I don't know what to do with others once they're around me.

I've accepted Wesley and the jogger. Flaws and age and all. Kudos to me. But I know I could be doing so much more by going for the jugular. Thinning the herd. Spacing out the question of what we are and how to be.

"Is this Stacy?"

"Yes," says Stacy.

"I'm a friend of your son's." What's that mean? "I'm...well, I'm a friend of Will's, your brother."

"Is this Lance?"

"Yeah. Yes. It is."

"Will's friend. Of course. I can't believe we've never talked." She sounds pleasant. Not at all like the neglectful mom I'd pictured for young Wesley. "Is everything okay?"

"Yes, and so is Wesley. He's...well. He's well."

"You know Wesley?" she asks, maybe proudly.

"Yes. We work together. Practically. I work for him, in a sense. I'm calling to..." Say it. Say *some*thing. To meet. To find a quiet place where no one would suspect your death. "Um...it's strange, honestly."

"Is Wes all right?"

"You call him Wes? Yes. He's fine. And Will. Both W's."

She doesn't laugh. She hears right through the phone holes and down the wire that I'm deranged.

"Are you okay?"

"Thank you. Yes." I like her. "I wanted, I guess, to hear your voice first. Obviously, since we're on the phone."

"Huh? Oh. Yes, that's true. That happens first, doesn't it?"

"Yeah. And, you know, you have a fine son. Your broseph, Will, is a bit much to handle." I laugh as people do. Heavy on the exhale, her cue to join me in the light bullying and healthy laughter.

"Yes. Will's a lot."

"But Wesley is a good lad." I laugh. She laughs. "He recently took me in. Helped me out. And...I suppose that's everything."

"Oh."

"I'll cross you off my list." One more laugh for good measure.

"Oh, okay. Well, thank you. I'm in the middle of some things right now, but I appreciate the call. Very kind."

She abruptly hangs up which causes me to hesitate before the cross off, possibly snatching the sounds and tones of her true colors at the end there, but the buzz inside me is killed. Ironic.

3ʳᵈ Sibling (Will's sister–Stacy)

For sure, she's going to tell Will and Wesley about the out-of-nowhere call from the freak friend. If any of them consider me one. Fuck, long-distance trials are crushing my get-up-and-go. Stopping over at Prey Pursuit is becoming too far of a destination. I can hardly hop aboard the murder train to begin with, my goddamn hip preventing me from moving forward (more than I'd like to admit). When does the motivational pull change from something ahead to something below? Naming it. Aware that I'm considering my own death-date. Not wanting to be grounded. Not wanting my physical ailments to knock me down in the meantime. Because I don't want to be leveled, sacked, crawling, or grasping at an ankle. I want the chase, man. And before it's too late, before I run out of steam and lose track of Destination Kill, before I'm bedridden from the surgery, I'm going to the doctor's office. And then the dentist. See if I still have a chance at living another day to stop someone else from living. I'm like a Bond villain with my own movie title: *Live Another Day to Stop Another's.*

The moped scoots me close to the door of the hospital, a gutted and remodeled home (to be fair to the realtor), and I go ahead and take the handicap spot. No lie there. Come and get me, coppers and nosey do-gooders.

I pull out my list like a map.

I'm on the Murdering Tours. Where's your bathroom and nearest machete?

> **Roshell**
> ~~**Jogger**~~
> ~~**Registration Bitch[es] (college)**~~
> ~~**Idiotic Clown Students (college)**~~
> **Dentist**
> ~~**Will**~~
> ~~**Will's nephew (Wesley)**~~
> **Paul (cousin)**
> ~~**Bruce (retired)**~~
> **Nurse (fuckable)**
> ~~**Elizabeth (Butt—Betty)**~~
> **Doctor (hip guy)**
> **Polish (woman)**
> **Wretched (???)**
> ~~**Coach (mine)**~~
> **Impatient (Golfer)**
> ~~**Other Golfer**~~
> **Bob**
> ~~**3rd Sibling (Will's sister—Stacy)**~~

I used to get hard by simply reading the word "fuckable." ("Piece of ass" never did it for me.) And seeking out the fuckable nurse after reading that? Fuck me. Please.

Yes, I'm looking for the fuckable nurse. No coercion. I need to be sure she's no longer a suspect for murder.

And when I say for murder, I mean to be murdered. Plain and simple.

"Can I help you?"

Another looker, too. Boy, am I close to saying all that.

"Is the doc in?"

"Which doctor were you looking for?"

I've forgotten his name, and I feel terrible about it. How can I feel bad about the guy I'd like to slice and dice with his own scalpel?

"Lance!" he says, coming around the corner like a racist depiction of a foreigner.

"Wow, doc, you remembered my name."

"I'm between patients. Take that how you like." I laugh. Not bad. "Are you here a day early?" I don't remember him being this spunky and funny. "Are you nervous?" There it is. The serious, concerned face. I remember *that* guy.

"I was in the neighborhood."

"Hmm." He's not too good at the receiving end of the unfunny-joke circle. "Do you want to come back for a quick sec?"

"Uh..."

"Come on back. Nurse, hold my calls. I'm just joking."

That was a miss, doc. Not even sure what the line carries beyond making me feel uncomfortable and old fashioned, searching my brain for a Three Stooges reference or something ancient and black and white. Something I'd rather leave behind when eyeing the place for a tasty nurse. God, this place even smells old. A covered-up kind of rotten.

He opens the hollow door that separates the lobby from the mini hall. It creaks like the basement-entrance scene of a horror flick. I don't think I've been to this house hospital. Is this where I'm scheduled for my hip fix? I suddenly get a hot flash rooted in stupidity and doubt and shame. Get a grip. The doctor's confirmed my appointment. I'm getting confused, is all.

"I was being funny earlier," I say. "Having never been here, to this office. I'm trying out the new wheels. Just bought me a moped." Am I committing my appointment, my presence, to memory?

"No. We—you, myself, and your wife—met at the hospital. Which is where you'll be having the procedure. This is my office. Half the week, I'm here."

"Right."

"You won't be coming here."

"Oh. Right. I looked up your address on the card."

"Yes. That's what it's there for. After you." He opens his palm as if the room were tiny and in the center of his hand.

Stress is jumbling my brain. That's okay. That happens. Concentration falters when under pressure.

Last time I was with the doc, I asked him personal questions. In general. I inquired about biting during sex. He didn't have an answer, yet, I kept at it. Asked if sexual gnawing was a predatory instinct. That scene ended with him putting me on the spot, asking if I chew the insides of my mouth or lips by accident when I eat. I thought of saying something about eating a woman's pussy and didn't, because I'm not cut from that low-class cloth, no matter what others may say or think. Instead, I said, "No. I don't bite the inside of my mouth by accident. I *consciously* bite the inside of my mouth." I didn't fess up to pulling his chain nor get specific and describe a nervous tic. I left the doc sitting on his circular stool at the center of misunderstanding, facetiousness, and elderly confusion.

"I'm really fine," I say.

"*Doctor* Fine?"

"What? Oh. No."

"Three Stooges."

"Yeah. I know. No."

"Good."

"I'm thinking things through."

"You're nervous."

"I'm seeking satisfaction in my last day. I guess." Where the hell did that come from?

"Do you believe you're going to die?"

"No."

"That's common. The thought. The result of death, however, is uncommon."

"Okay. Good. That's good. Not why I'm here, though."

"Okay. Great. Why are you here?"

That's the spot. That's the angle of the interaction. The soul-crushing communication squeeze. Where we get lost. Where we feel like we're dumped on, or less than enough, or not enough something. I know I have the ability to squash his head like fresh bread. I droop into a scared, cold feeling. Cool on the skin but tingling deep to my ribs. At the center of the bones, rushing up and down them like thick water, is room-temperature ice. I should be nauseous. I'm not. The body's resistance comes from the same place. A good body tackle or smashing of the gas pedal normally helps me plow through it, and the bones above my gut get hard, and the inside flowing melts into hot spit (but not in the mouth). Heartburn would taste just right. Blood could drip from my gums or nose. I'd handle the moment and this creep.

"Are you feeling dizzy?"

"Yeah," I say and lean back. He helps me, lean or fall or neither.

"You've grown pale."

"Grown?"

"When did you last eat?"

"Last eat? Eat last?"

"Yes."

"I skipped, maybe?"

"I hope not. Not with that hip." I'm able to snicker. So I'm okay. "Are you with me?"

"Yeah," I say. "Where else would I be?" He smiles with no joy. "I was thinking too hard."

His "heh" is a very loud type of laugh and startles me.

"I'm going to call out for the nurse, but don't take it as an insult. I'm only asking for water and some crackers. For you."

"And a sticker. And a sucker," I say in place of "a tight ass."

Nice folks here. Crackers are excellent. A regular two-piece, name-brand package. Orange juice, too. Strong, tasty. Also name-brand. They had an electrolyte drink to-go. All for free. All without an appointment. All for my care.

He wished me well. He trusted I was all right. I trust he's an alright man. Most of the nurses were not very attractive, and I never got to see the fuckable one from before. They can't all be winners. And let's leave that world as is, Lance.

Get to the dentist before five, and try not to pass out. You've got assessments to make. Places to go, people to kill.

No appointment. Dentist comes out to say hello. I express concern about my crooked mouth-opening he'd once mentioned in passing. He sits me in the wavy chair, no problem. An impromptu jaw check before they close for the day.

"Thanks for this," I say. "I didn't expect you to—"

"Are you wearing the mouth piece?"

I explain that I've lost it. He expresses concern and the idea to schedule an appointment.

Like the doctor's office, I'm not getting any kind of satisfaction from the female help. I envision a dental slaughter. Crazily massacring the people I've come across in the waiting room, the new patients I passed by today, and those whom I, realistically, didn't expect to run into (for example, the Polish woman from my last visit). The dentist-office people are not very interesting. Probably not worth my wrath. Not because I'm losing my nerve. They just don't fit into my ideal Death Day. I'm more disappointed and agitated about not making my mark at this particular location than flat-out angry by professionalism and appointment talk.

"Thank you for checking," I say on the way out. "I didn't expect that."

"I like the moped."

"Thanks, doc."

And I *brrrrrmm* off. No helmet. At my age, a higher-level rebel maneuver.

I'll have to make a poop stop before home, and the return to the record store is convenient, but I bet this stopover is also an attempt to seek a place of nowhere to master the funk I'm in.

Since I'm here, I'll make sure there's no one worth killing.

The overhead disco distracts. Never been a fan. A customer gets too close. I say, "Fuck the disco-tech," because I think he's around my age, maybe fifteen years younger. He smiles like he understands but appears afraid. Good. Fear it all, yuppie. (What's the term for an old yuppie?)

I suddenly think of the lines from Sinatra's "Young at Heart" and the night they sunk into my chest, melting and hardening there for years. Last time I was here, I stated how irritating Sam Cooke's voice becomes at the end of "Everybody Likes to Cha Cha Cha." Jeffrey and Ryan debunked my opinion. Said I was overreacting. I've just become sick of that part because I've been hearing it for so many years, they said. That's happened to them with other songs. I argued that the level of my despising hadn't risen. My irritation hadn't expanded. In that moment, I was remembering how I always hated Cooke's going on and on in that particular song. It wasn't a current annoyance. And I thought of the times when I was cross with others. I thought of radiation. I thought of mingling and all the years I've mingled. And I made a joke, connecting my wrinkles to pain. Jeffrey and Ryan laughed, and it wasn't funny. I thought of the time I defended myself to Betty and how things I tend to hate don't always cause skin crinkles. Not everything grows as a fungus or mold in the crevices of my body. Some things are crap right off the bat. And they don't stick to you like goddamn ageless glue. I've always hated how Cooke sounded during the fade out, but I can still appreciate his voice and other songs. Cooke's been the white man's black man forever. That may sound racist to some people, but I don't think so. I wasn't even the one who claimed this during the conversation.

I'm thinking hard about this, recalling how badly I wanted to mention how depressing it was to see James Brown and Al Green in the 1990's, when a customer nods my way to be polite. I don't want that. I also don't want to be questioned by Jeffrey or Ryan or anyone else. I said I was taking a break and have returned after only a few days. I know this and that it doesn't make sense. Now, leave me the hell alone about it. Because I'm not a working retiree. It's a stupid concept stupid people fall into, and I'm not doing it. I'm not stupid. Stepping foot into this yuppie, hippie, hipster, thrasher, alternative crap-place confirms the pointlessness. How meaningless this job and this part of my life was. I somehow, however, don't regret trying it out. A sixteen-year-old go-getter or a nineteen-year-old dropout can experiment with shitty jobs. So can an older gentleman such as myself. I worked and stopped without giving up on some harebrained dream or career. No long-term ideas took over. I just quit going. My right to do so. Homelessness, if I'd ever succumb to that, can be freeing. I don't know where I'm going with that thought, but it's connected to the others in some way.

Also, not being able to play an instrument repetitively irked me when in this place. I've picked up some guitars over the course of my life. I've messed with a girlfriend's piano. (A good girl, that one was. She played here and there. Something about her posture and tits made her work at those keys genuine. I was really into her bad fingering. But she wasn't into mine.)

From the register near the entrance, I wave to an unfamiliar employee entering the back room and remove the dentist/doctor office possibilities from the list.

> ~~Dentist~~
> ~~Nurse (fuckable)~~
> ~~Doctor (hip guy)~~
> ~~Polish (woman)~~

I rewrite a shortened version with some paper from the counter, squeeze my ass cheeks to control the exit hole, and take off with the final murderee suspects in hand.

CHAPTER 22

I'm proud to say I've never been one to question or wallow in the land of Misery by saying, "So this is where I've ended up, huh?" but am close to it when taking a dump between two grown men in a loud café across from the record store, feeling and hearing the arthritic pop of my wrist when I wipe my ass, complimented by the quiet creaks of my left hand's three middle fingers I jammed ten years ago (awaiting a full healing point along with the chronically-cramping middle toes on my right foot).

Being unable to keep in my shit for the home bathroom is something that used to happen. End of the day, and I'm in a sweaty, sphincter panic (if not a panic over a sweaty sphincter). Having to make a pit stop on the fly like this is something different. More concerning, I guess. And I have lengthier poops at this age, in terms of allocating time to the solo sit-down and not the size of the poo itself.

In my youth, I would've entertained the idea of masturbating in the stall after catching sight of all those beautiful women in the café line. No desire to ask or take them to bed because it'd spoil the fantasy. Even though my experienced interactions have been worth it, sometimes, lots of times. I'd catch myself imagining life-long scenarios or events that didn't involve commitment or long-lasting relationship status. And this isn't a current, age-related lack of yearning due to a lack of testosterone. No, a more accurate example of losing inhibitions with age (at my age) is how we sound off a warning. Like verbalizing, "Get out while you still have a chance!" before dropping your drawers to crap in a public café men's room. Or forget the words. Blow a tremendous fart into the bowl to let the men know where you stand (sit). I've done that, too, during my many years on this space ball of public-bathroom users.

I'm feeling witty. Sometimes the case when expelling from the rear.

At one of the café tables, I was fortunate to observe a group of seven-to-eight lively pre-eighteen-year-old girls silently managing gut laughter. Red faces and open mouths covered by delicate hands. Their eyes darted back and forth within their darkened sockets, contrasted by the glowing social circle that was unable to contain the hilarity of witnessing something grand, exciting, and fun.

I wanted to be a part of their laughter. It wasn't youth I was seeking. It (I) was missing out on the moment. I felt inclined to take the two steps necessary to get closer and ask, "What's so funny?" but didn't. Sad we can't do that. Fifty-some years ago, a hippie would have involved anyone around to spread the joy, love, and grass. He also may have had taken advantage of the weakest chick there. Not my intention.

As I stood my ground as an outsider, I spotted the water that must have spilled on the table and one of the girl's chests. I smiled. "Can you get us some napkins, please?" one of them asked me, containing new roars the best she could.

I don't know why, but I looked away. I didn't assist them. I couldn't bring myself to be a part of the moment. In those few seconds, it was important I be less vital or useful than the employee who ultimately fetched them napkins. By staying out of it, I'd be revered less than any of the younger adults there. Maybe not. But maybe so. I didn't want to take the chance. They were beautiful, as humans are. I didn't want to taint any of that with my presence and reality. My age.

I'm lost in the comprehension of the thing, feeling far less intellectual than a moment ago.

Before I know it, I'm straddling my moped out front. Watching an ancient woman maneuver out from a wide parking spot. No other cars. No people. No light poles. She's cautious and, yet, nearly tears off her rear bumper, barely missing the wall before the lot's exit. Am I capable of making that kind of mistake? Do I drive like that? Walk like that? Talk like that? Am I a person with low competency?

How does she shit?

The lady with the swinging handicap sign is mirroring an internal reflection, one I'd like to cover with a king-sized bedsheet. Even out here, sitting on this toy-like bike at the left of the setting sun and cool wind, listening to the my motor stutter, watching all the no-nonsense zoom around me, permitted to drive amongst them, I can't escape myself and restrictions.

Because I know I'm not as good as I once was at taking turns and predicting depth of field. In a car, I can be a mess. Big of me to admit, I'd say. I'm not quite at the stage where I'd qualify for the mandate or law I always complain about us needing (to put something in place that'd take licenses away from dangerous, blind oldies, which I thought about saying at a town council meeting but know I'd never set foot in one), but I've got limitations.

This lady needs that handicap symbol permanently stamped onto her license plate, because the plastic one on the rearview mirror isn't cutting it. Add a ring of neon lights around the pictograph. A siren to knock back anyone within fifteen feet. I don't know if this would impede on rights, but fuck it. They'd be my rights, too. Take 'em away.

Surprise, surprise, I'm not feeling that biker freedom vibe from the moped. I'm feeling like the laughingstock of my surroundings. Exposed as all hell.

I pull over to an empty parking lot. Check the new, revised list. Meant to do it on the shitter. Forgetful ass.

> **Roshell**
> **Paul (cousin)**
> ~~Wretched (???) [don't remember]~~
> **Impatient (Golfer)**
> **Bob**

The crisp whiteness of the sheet bothers me, and I realize the briefer version of the possible kills unintentionally maps out locations I plan to visit after my surgery (in no particular order): drop by the golf course, go to Will's place (to find Bob), invite Roshell over for a one-on-one, and meet up with my cousin somewhere remote to give him the time of his life (he being suicidal leaves such a phrase open for layers of interpretation).

I'm dozing to *Carlito's Way*. Betty's feet on my lap. Al Pacino's character, Carlito, saying he didn't just one day decide to kill. That it doesn't work that way.

But what if your urge to kill is long overdue? What if your deep dream (or pride or satisfaction or strange idea at which others will laugh) is to kill someone? Because you can. Because it's your time now.

My inner motives to kill are symbolic: inferiority complex (feeling old in comparison to new generations); self-hatred (for allowing myself to age); and fear of death (hating myself for having an inferiority complex).

I can't mention any of this to Betty because she read my memoirs. I've exposed myself before I've exposed myself. And isn't that what Carlito is saying? He messed up and showed his true colors because of his upbringing. Or he's attempting to let loose now, everyone chuckling at his idea to sell cars. When can he be the man he wants to be? And we know he doesn't reach his dream. We know he dies in the end because they reveal it at the beginning.

Why show that? What's this movie telling us? Life's short? Death's inevitable? Dreams are false? Dreams are only dreams? Is there no one out there who yearns to take a life as a personal challenge or achievement? Do I have to look at my past to justify such an act? I have to be pushed? Brought to the precipice?

"Hey," she says, waking me up. The movie's still playing but somehow only a few seconds further into the picture. "You were tapping your hand like a nut."

"Sorry."

"Were you sleeping?"

"Getting there."

It's not about survival of the fittest. The streets. The codes. The trauma. It's about being yourself, wholly. No holding back.

"I don't know," I say. "I think you can decide for yourself. Make yourself be something."

"What? You're sleep talking."

In the mirror, I've never seen myself in a veteran hat. Does that mean I wasn't chosen? I was rejected? Do I, then, make myself a certain way? Make up for that void? Any and all voids? Does a mirror hold everything you're not? How big of a piece of shit you actually are? Why, sometimes, it might be better to give up? On anything? On life? Is killing yourself better than killing someone else? Is that why so many off themselves after a murdering spree? Why the fuck is it called a spree? Why isn't that word used for anything else besides killing and shopping?

"Some Sprees would be good right now," I say to prove I'm awake. "Watching the movie. Having some candy."

"You'd choke in the middle of a nod off, bozo."

I don't ever consider killing myself. That's never been my go-to or style. I wonder if this is my first suicidal thought.

I know I felt deep hopelessness when Betty and I were in our third year of marriage and already fighting. Wild fighting between two gray-headed sons of bitches felt like too much. But out of that, there was never an attempt to die by my own hand. If anything, we made a promise to each other to put less pressure on ourselves whenever anniversaries and Valentine's Days and birthdays would arrive. Celebrate every day. Some days would mean more than others, because we'd make them so. That's all. As a matter of fact, that deal's been working and hasn't been broken from either end since it was put into place.

I'm worthy. Betty's worthy. We create our worth.

Fuck suicide. Fuck my cousin and his weak jackass mentality.

CHAPTER 23

I'm dying. In a whirlwind. A tunnel. Through it, out of it, stuck in it, crawling like a baby, rolling like an invalid. An old man. A *dying* old man. The very thing, the very type of human, I'm refusing. I'm where I'm refusing, inside the refusal, the quicksand, part of the neglect and avoidance and ignorance and nothingness. I'm the kid I was. I'm the dead I'm not. But I am.

But I'm not.

Coming around, getting clearer in my head or body–no, in my head. My head, cleaning up the past, swept out from it, over the dustpan, into some dusty, smoke-like light. The place of back then, where I had to be quiet. Where kids were shit. Nothing. Girls meant to obey, boys meant to grow up. We, all of us, were beaten. Many...No, I wasn't beaten. That's a lie. My father asked for a punch to the face. A kick to the balls.

Is that my hand? My body? Because I'm here.

Wasn't I on the couch? *Carlito's Way*?

I was there during the reign of the .44 Killer. Son of Sam. I was thirty maybe. It was my birthday. Or around it. I remember–the memory getting cleaner as I approach–how connected I felt or wanted to feel in the 70's when reading the letters Killer Sam had sent the newspapers. Not that I wanted to dish out anything to decode. Not to be a copycat and skip through people's puddles of dread in fear-mongering rain boots. No. A different connection. A *real* connection. I wanted to talk to the so-called maniac. Have a lunch break with him. Eat with dirty hands on the rooftop of a neighborhood house we'd repair.

I went through the same elation when I read the Unabomber's letters. And that fella was right in my own backyard. A Michigander reaching out for another who would understand. I wanted to watch that guy make a sandwich in his shack home.

There's something about grubbing with these men. Breaking bread. Having a beer. Shooting the shit and, after munching, *literally* shooting up some shit. Not feces. Some world "turds." Rap-a-tap-tapping the shitty shit-eaters off the ground, up into the air, and out of town. Because there was something to that, wasn't there? Getting an empty can to do what you want, just by smacking it with a bullet. Getting it to linger in the air. Like the hat shooting in the cowboy movies with Eastwood. Or pushing through a crowd at a Beatles concert. Never did that. But nonsensical chaos, pushing those people into the railings, intrigued me.

The Beatles' "I'll Get You" is a perfect example of the Emotional Classifieds through which I sometimes thumb. My last year of high school. That song screaming at me. Inside me. From inside out. I'd shout with John. To get the girl. To collect her. Not control or defile, but engulf. Possess. Or maybe just terrify. Get someone to notice you're terrified of yourself.

In the end, I'll get you, alright!

Feeling some kind of ecstasy in my loins. A love song that got me feeling hard and dark before it was cool for movies to mismatch music and scenes. The 80's have since made music-box tinkles eerie. Happy, pop songs are best utilized against cinematic bloodbath shootouts. The art of satire has become satirical in itself, if you ask me.

But, sure, charging through a Beatles crowd. Smashing the front row into the barriers. Or knocking bodies down from up high, off a cliff. Off a rooftop. Peter Pan and Superman jumpers. Something arousing there.

People could storm us like pod people or zombies, and we'd take them all down. Me and my killer friends. Kings of the hill. Kings of the kill.

Is there something noble in making it through that anarchy? Something powerful? Empowering? Like a lone Spartan slashing away at the lofty, hanging branches of droopy leaves? Stupid, droopy-faced morons. (But Droopy, the cartoon dog, was intelligent as hell. He was no bitch.) I don't know. I'm trying to make sense of making sense. Why I desire certain things. And I always think I missed my chance with the Zodiac Killer. In my early twenties at the time. Not as interested (as I am now?) in death or taking lives. Or the people who took them. Does *that* mean anything?

I'm uncomfortable.

The losers of this world always want someone to blame, but they only have themselves. To blame, that is. And I'm the one to show them that, to give them someone to blame. That is me. The one to blame. For killing them, that is I. I'm the one to blame for them getting themselves killed. Because, in turn, they're the ones to blame for being stupid enough to get killed. A complete circle.

I thump the hospital bed. Solid. Understanding where I am. The foundation beneath me. A recovery room and not my couch of watery, drowning sand.

Three weeks of this dreamland continue and diverge and merge into one direction. Sleep and awake, dreaming and rationalizing as a single, crisscrossed path.

Where I am today, thoughts and body in my home, is similar to where I was three weeks ago, coming out of the anesthesia. Lost in thoughts, now found. Daily, knowing my determination to end another's life, that goal, is more righteous and necessary because of my new perspective.

Nothing matters when you come back from going under. No, I take that back. I think it's everything matters more. The nothingness of the world *also* matters. And that's got to be dealt with. The nothingness people carry, on and on. Generation after generation.

These rude awakenings, awakening my rude side as opposed to others rudely stirring me from a deep sleep, are common. Altogether, they make up my base mood.

I wonder: could my rudeness—what is claimed as rude by a rude society—simultaneously open its own eyes and see me while pulling me out of a sloshy slumber?

I've been ruminating. Healing. Bettering myself. Strengthening and planning to take life by someone else's balls, finally deciding the death will be that of a man. I won't physically touch the guy's nuts, of course. Maybe I'm considering the action crass to balance the respect I have for the finer sex's genitalia and not grabbing at it.

The machine Betty and I purchased is good for upper-body strength. Easier on the hips. Building what I've got. Maintaining without taking strenuous walks. Exactly what I alluded to for the jogger's benefit.

Nevertheless, I'm on an early walk.

Feel the breeze. Feel the sidewalk. Acknowledge your place in the world, man. Come on, Lance. Get with it. Pull your head out of your ass. Your hip's bionic now. You're the elder superhero: Mega Mature. You've got a second chance. Quickly, you have the notion of being a villain, that that's more accurate a description, but that's not right either. Killing isn't exclusive for the bad. Cops, the army, comic book heroes with guns, Rambo (After the movie, I read *First Blood* and was put in a mood for weeks.), Schwarzenegger, countries, hunters, the meek with rocks and stones, the frail little girl in the corner who wins by fighting back. You've got a new hip. You've got a second coming. Yes, you've said that, and you're saying it again. Come at the world with a fist. A balled-up, creased, veiny, liver-spotted fist. Fuck yeah!

When I get back home from my stroll, I plow through the front door. Feeling like a million bucks. I could probably give it to Betty as I did on our first date.

"Betty?!"

"Mr. Fancy Pants over here," says Will from the couch, feet propped up on the chair like a wise guy looking for money, "says the only thing people want out of life is satisfaction. Comfort. To increase or maintain pleasure and reduce or get rid of pain and uncomfortableness. Stress and all that. You know. But I asked him about rapists. And that's when Bob gave me some crap about compulsions and that there are healthier ways to engage in sex. And that the rapist is getting pleasure from the pain. His own inner turmoil. Did I get that right? That's what you said, Bobby? Because, really, it's control or rage the rapist is trying to get or—what was it—manage?"

I'm uncomfortable, out of sorts, vulnerable, unprepared. Where the fuck is Bob? Behind the door?! Really, Bob, you're hiding? Peek-a-booing?

And since I'm startled as a son of a bitch, I wonder if Bob noticed the evil grin (for lack of a more original description of my showing inners) I was wearing when I entered the room.

"Where's Betty?" I ask. I nod to Bob's presence like a weakling.

"She said you have to get out of the house," says Will. "You're not kicked out, but you need a routine."

"Oh." I look at Bob's nodding head and say, "Did she tell you about the stationary bike we dusted off? And the new machine?"

"Nah," Will interrupts.

"Working on the upper body?" Bob asks like a demon reading thoughts. Because he's not an angel. I know. "Stationary equipment is great. Less reliance on the lower back or hip."

"This is Bob's last day in town. So what do you think?"

"About?" I ask.

"We're taking your butt out to golf. Betty said you mentioned it again, so you don't have a say in that. But I'm talking about Fancy Pants Bobby Boy. Saying how we only want pleasure. How I stumped him and his crap-knowledge on rape."

I look to Bob. Is he going to defend himself? Take the bait? Nope. And Will already knew that. Brotherly bullshit. Am I in the mood for that?

I narrow in on Bob's eyes. Maybe because it's his last day in town. Maybe because I've mastered my walk and my brand-spanking-new hip. Maybe because I was thinking about Rambo. Or do I lock onto Bob's eyes because I'm being bushwhacked, momentarily distracted by the word "ambushed," thinking how both "ambushed" and "bushwhacked" are synonyms for "attack" and involve "bush" and how "bushwhacking" seems manlier, probably because women say they're getting "ambushed" by men while men like to whack bushes with their dicks?

My eyes never leaving Bob's, I say, "What about murder?"

Will of course comes back with, "What about it?"

But I'm not asking him. I'm asking Bob.

"Bob," I say, minus the pretentious one-eyebrow raise of a British scoundrel. "There's no healthy replacement for murder."

"War," Bob overlaps and continues, rapid fire. "Survival. Protecting one's family."

"Protection," I nod, advocating for the devil with slow accuracy. "One's family. One's country. One's liberty. Protecting yourself."

"One could say," says Bob, "those justify another's death."

"Murder," I emphasize. "Not death. I'm saying murder."

"Maybe I'm not understanding the question."

"I think you do."

"Fuck off, Bob, you get it," Will interjects, assuring us he hasn't left the room. "Lance is saying there's not a satisfying, moral pleasure to murder."

"No," I say, adamant as hell, "that's not my point. Murder is satisfying to many. To murderers, in fact. Not gangbangers. Not in self-defense. There is a natural, uh—"

"Innate?" Bob assists.

"*Innate* pleasure for premeditated, depraved murderers."

"Premeditat*ing*," Bob corrects me.

"I knew he was going to correct something you said, Lance," Will sides, feet dropping from the couch armrest to the carpet.

"Because," Bob explains, "a murderer is actively premedi*tating*. Planning. Considering. Forward-thinking. A premedi*tated* murder, on the other hand, has happened. There was a purpose before it. Death is now present. Created. Mastered. Completed."

"The deed is done," Will adds, trying to wrap it up.

"And, to add," Bob continues, "premeditation is not necessarily the same as modus operandi, where the deed is particular to the person."

"Show off," Will says, getting up and heaving out his age in a grunt. He's bored and opens the front door for our communal exit.

"There's pleasure in the hunt," Bob says.

"That's what I'm saying," I say. "As there is for a detective."

To me, Will says, "Betty said you two have been watching a lot of Hitchcock."

"We watched *Apt Pupil* the other day."

"I don't know that one," Bob says.

"There's that line," I say, "where the old man says people don't understand the power there is in not killing someone, knowing he can kill anyone at any time."

"Is that Hitchcock?" Will asks.

"Stephen King," I answer. "Based on a short story."

Bob's watching me. Watching me watch him. In his head, probably watching himself watch me. How he does what he does. I won't let him get me lost in his head, though. I won't be bushed in any form.

"So, do you agree?" I ask. "Is there pleasure, innate pleasure, in murder?"

"No," says Bob, looking away, rolling the ball with the string so I can pounce like some tiny-brained feline. He actually has a golf ball in his hand, I realize. Why the hell–? "No one derives pleasure from a principle that causes chaos. The true murderer doesn't want to look over his shoulder."

"He doesn't want to be murdered," Will translates, now on my porch.

"Nor does he want to be caught and, yes, Will, the killer could be avoiding spending multiple years, or life, in prison. Possibly sentenced to death. Murdered by the state. Not to make this conversation political."

"It's not," Will defends us against no one listening.

"The pleasure in murder," concludes Bob, "is to alleviate one's pain. To alleviate the pain of one's painful life."

And Will says what I'm thinking: "There's no death penalty in Michigan."

CHAPTER 24

I'm certain I hate golf. I don't have the patience for the sport of inner-peace and serenity. And not only have I fallen into this mental state before, I've physically walked this course with these same two fools. Bored out of my fucking mind.

Somewhere in the air, I hear a familiar tune. I air-guitar with a 7-iron. Never have I done that. Proof of how jaded and uninterested I am. As out of character as the baseball hat I wore last time on the green.

I regret pulling out the club. I regret Will's laughter. I regret never learning guitar. I regret crying through those few months of kindergarten piano lessons and quitting. I regret leaving (and meeting) that girl who played the piano, because of my deep admiration for her tits and personality. I know this to be true. And I don't want to wonder or debate if she was The One. The one who got away. I don't want to ask myself if I scared her off by being myself. If we simply didn't fully connect or if it was something else. I'm too old to fall into a Scrooge-like memory of bitterness. Or am I just the right age for that? I could have been kinder to that girl. Married her. Gave her babies. Cheated on her. Apologized. Raised my hand and never smacked her. Cried one time because she said something that involved, I don't know, my parents not understanding that I wasn't a real leader. She could have been my love. The only one who could have known how to hurt me.

I wouldn't have cheated on her. Not that one.

Wandering over manmade fields, having nothing better to do but get lost in thought and convince myself of no regrets, is really depressing and another reason I hate this game. It's sucking the suck out of sucking, as Ryan used to say. The ultimate suck.

I shouldn't be reviewing the past.

I should be reviewing my kills.

> **Roshell**
> **Paul (cousin)**
> ~~**Wretched (???) [don't remember]**~~
> **Impatient (Golfer)**
> **Bob**

I still don't know who the hell Impatient was. A golfer, I get. But who? Not that guy I threw the ball at. If I happen to come across Impatient (some member in a polo and white pants, I'm assuming), maybe I'll grow a pair of ripe-old cojones and get a kill. Recall how antsy his panties are and knock him dead with a nice drive–club or golf cart.

"Whoa! That's a slice of lime!" Will comments on my hooked ball.

"Who gives a shit?" I say.

Bob does. Because he says, "Things aren't always what someone says they are."

"Uh, Lance hit the ball for it to go straight, and it didn't. Pretty straightforward." Will laughs at himself. "Ha! Get it?"

"Perhaps, something like hitting a golf ball isn't simple. As simple as a slice. When from another angle, it is."

"Alright, Bob. You're saying something can be something and not something. Okay. Very good observation. Majorly intuitive there."

"If we truly knew," Bob drones on, completely self-aware, "we'd also be certain whether or not chicken breasts swell when you cook them."

And he takes a swing. Pulled the ball out of his pocket

like a pervert magician and swung with an iron. Not even a wood! And I don't know what the hell he means. Breasts? Balls in his pocket? Is it all a ploy to see if I'll respond sexually? Like a Rorschach for Dummies? No wood?

Bob isn't some wise, proficient detective. He's a fake. A phony cop. A less-than-qualified investigator. I'm finally looking through him, and he doesn't know dick about being a dick. Nothing but an old fart visiting and playing 9 holes with his brother and his brother's half-friend. Shooting the shit. Putt-putzing around the green. Thinking he's above par. Searching for a hole in one. Planting his flag. Acting like he owns this town and the course.

I think he's a good example of a rambling old man. No longer apt to handle the ever-changing world. A symbol of the generation gap. Something I'm not and never have been.

"Did he say chicken breasts swell?" Will whispers to me. "Lance, you okay?"

"Will...you...shut up?"

Will smiles. I return the mouth behavior so we can get on with it. To the next hole.

"Your swing."

I swing. Goddamn aware. Like Bob. But above this golf crap and cryptic conversations about chicken breasts and not knowing what's what (not knowing what the hell Bob's going on about).

Come, Bob. *Come smile with me, let's smile, let's smile away.* Show teeth. Come see if you can master my mind. Because I don't think you can. Perhaps, you once knew how. But I think you're slightly senile. Not the wise man you think you are. You've lost the skill. Your clout with your department (what Will informed me of before you joined us today) and with me? The game between you and me? You've lost. You've lost to me, and you don't even know it.

"You're positive you're okay?" Will asks me, near my body, friendly like.

"What's the problem?"

"Your face, man. You have a crooked version of your regular resting-ass face."

"Resting what?" I ask.

Bob smirks.

Did I just get played? Or left out of a slang exchange?

Generation gaps happen when a person has less interaction with the new generation, or the next generation, or the one after that. Will, though, is also an old man and wouldn't know how to close any gaps.

I was somewhere between fifty and sixty when a friend of mine croaked. The funeral was just before the turn of the century, back when everyone was panicking about computers failing, unable to correctly code for the 2000's. The deceased's older brother (by five years) spoke like a beatnik. For as long as I'd known him, saying stuff like "corny" and "gas" and "cat," annunciating the root and alterations of the words. The times of the words. He wore a toupee atop some real, hanging, ponytailed hair.

What I'm getting to is, no matter the words used, I've had something loose in my skull that stops me from fitting with any Generation Speak at any time. But my oddball approach has solely been mine. No one can take that. Nor from me.

"Hole nine already?" Bob announces, questioning our entire existence.

"Time get away from you, there, Bob?" I ask.

"I'm wondering if we should have shot eighteen."

"Lance can't handle that," Will jokes, poking me in the butt with his club.

"Get out of here!" I'm clenching my fists. The handle went right up my asshole.

Too angry. Too much. I've spoiled the green. I've exposed the thoughts, the disgust, the judgments, the privacy of my building and stacking. The pieces to protect from attacks and destruction. Like a tower of solid righteousness. Power from within that I mustn't reveal nor allow anyone to crash through!

Occupy the brain. Plan. Just as Bob the boob said: premeditate. What's my MO? My pattern? My gap?

I'm not interested enough to ask again. I turn my thoughts as I turn my wrist. This is my last tee-off. Like a countdown.

"I appreciate the exhale on the swing," says Bob.

I was the first to go, I realize. I'd been going last. I've cut in line.

My upbringing and the Monster of Courtesy inside forces me to apologize. Our collective upbringing allows us all to understand I've unconsciously moved ahead from my place, my position of being last, for no reason other than being absentminded.

Will waves my apology away as Bob closes his eyes and nods, ingesting my words.

I pretend to watch as they take their swings.

Back to private thoughts.

Questioning my MO. The three motives to kill: money, love, and revenge. Knowing I'm not interested in any of these. I'm not in need of money or love. And there's no status threatened, so revenge against whom? The youth? All of them?

I suppose there's a love for, and a loss of, the past. But I won't kill over regret. What's more interesting is my long-lost love to kill. Never fulfilled.

The point is I should be aware of the basic tidbits behind a murderous need beyond selfish desire. The basics of who, what, when, where, why, and how should be apparent.

I've narrowed down the subjects to a shortlist. That's the *who*.

The *what*? A van. Does that answer that? Or what to kill with? I'm coming around to the idea of choking with my bare hands.

When? At night. Or maybe first thing in the morning.

Where? Is that also the van? I may really need to check out a dealership. *Where* could also define the location of the crime and the drop-off point (where to leave the body). I should keep it local.

Why? Why not? You should try everything once.

To strike someone down. To feel excited and have a sense of purpose. Maybe that's not normal determination, but it's a feeling. Feeling persistence. Or persistent? Prepared to punch back. Take what's yours and smack it around. Like a judge with a mallet. Like a lumberjack with an axe. Maybe with a sledgehammer. Or one of those clown hammers from the strongest-man-alive carnival attraction. Like a god.

I picture a cop busting blacks on the head. Police knocking hippies around. News footage. Movies. Fake but real. Enough realism for me, since I've never been to a riot nor raised a sign for a cause. All these years, and I've never seen that kind of violence. I've witnessed fights. I've fought. I've punched my dad. That fucking memory sticking out again.

Yeah, I'm sure I'm getting there. To what I want to do. *How* I want to do it.

Bob's watching.

Will, hold me back. I feel like I'm in high school. Scrutinized. Pushed. Steaming mad.

I want to say something smart to Bob. Like a punk kid from today or my time. Like all those little shits and losers I've seen act tough through all those different decades. Thinking they know what strength is. I want to be like that but authentic.

"Game over," I say.

In silence, we've made it to the parking lot. Every one of us lollygagging.

"We goin' or what, baby?" Will asks Bob, leading us out.

"What's with the cutesy talk?" I ask. These two guys acting like a couple of lovers. I guess part of the brotherly connection I don't understand. A baby boomer without the boom. That's me. Always been me. A lone child amongst many. A reject from the orphans, bastards, and families. An only child who doesn't get to practice sibling deaths or aging, being in his seventies, working through and adjusting brain scrambles like a noir radio program.

"I was wondering the same thing," Bob says, grinning at my face for the first time.

From yards behind me, Will says, "Bob."

Bob, never moving his head, eyes on his brother: "Will."

And that's it. They've said their goodbyes to each other.

"Say bye-bye to Lance," Will says.

Bob's smile isn't as wide for me. I, however, sneer like the Joker. From the 60's show. Or maybe I'm the Riddler. That entire cast was straight out of a snuff film, wasn't it? Penguin the producer. Catwoman the pornstar. Robin the barely-legal. Directed by Alfred in his butler bowtie and underpants.

Man, I was all for the wild anarchy of Joker before his philosophical motivation was popularized. Before movies and characters became as strange and sinister as they did by the 2000's, I was already there. I'd been there. Today, I'm a retro killer. Understanding the menaces of society, connecting the dots from Dennis the menace to Bart Simpson to me before anyone else could see it. The interesting things I'd heard about *American Psycho* caused the same close-to-home curiosity I felt when Ted Bundy was caught (not so with Jeffrey Dahmer). The strange and unusual of Tim Burton movies. *Natural Born Killers* (which should have been at the top of my movie list titles, thinking back). The smashing of the gook's head in *Platoon*. Stephen King books being worse and more demented than the movie versions. Rambo's motivation in the novel. I was there, in it, all along. Swimming in thickness. Backstroking in that quicksand, the slop you shouldn't struggle against. Because being weighed down in it is an illusion. A falsity. I knew that. I knew about the dark side before *Star Wars* and, yet, never deemed that end of the spectrum as dangerous. I was into the original *Scarface*, interested in the sadistic tyrants and tormenters and wise guys in those pictures before they'd become anti-hero protagonists (or whatever the young ones were saying that day at the record store) by the 1980's. I'm before Jack Torrance's head-lowered gaze. To me, mental institutions were intriguing before the scandalous exposures. I fucking knew what kind of crazy those off-the-wall Bogart roles were rooted in.

True crime is a fucking fad. It's panic. It's entertainment for stupid people.

I'm more than that. I'm more than Bob. *I'm more than you*, I'm thinking, looking, staring, smiling, saying my goodbye like a goddamn gentleman with a revolver in his pocket.

Come on, Bob. One last time. In the parking lot. Let's meet toe to toe. Let's make Edward G. Robinson proud. A nice exit scene. A good dialogue piece. Play me like a fiddle. See if you're the mastermind you think you are. Put me in the hot seat. Do your worst, your best. Lay it on me. Lay it on thick. A street brawl before you go. Pretty please?

Wesley tears into the lot like a monster truck, the rumbling engine replaced with an electric wheeze. A spooky, fast approach from our future. "Hey, Lance!" I can't listen or greet until I get my footing. Because I'm in the middle of a match. I need to beat Bob at everything.

I shout, "A bat into hell," because he's entered the area. I sound like a crazy person.

"You ready," Wesley asks Bob.

I say, "Your Uncle's going to close his eyes and nod."

Maybe it's trying two lines in a row, or the surprise of Wesley's arrival, or something else, but I've done it. I've knocked Bob on his ass. Not literally. We're all standing here, saying our "see yas," shaping our lips to go up and back into more smiles. But Bob's been exposed. Will's never openly spoken of his brother's lame head movement, how Bob makes acknowledgments without words, or actions, or emotions only to close his fucking eyes like a goddamn freak.

But I hold onto this judgment and berating. Because I'm winning. I've won, haven't I, Bobby?

Wesley says, "Off to the airport," and takes the bag of clubs from Bob and hands them to Will, because they're borrowed. Bob's now standing there with nothing. His luggage already in the trunk. Nothing for this false detective to do but duck into the tiny, silently-idling car and leave the scene. Case unsolved. The murderer standing right here in front of him. A waste of time. Nothing for nothing.

Bob extends his hand to me. I take it.

"See you, Lance," Wesley says, getting back in the car, breaking my stare.

In one move, Bob swiftly releases my hand, turns away, opens the passenger door, and slips into Wesley's ride. He gazes past me and Will at the green fields.

"People say," Bob delivers like a setup, "prepackaged breast meat shrinks."

Will laughs hysterically. He'd be a better Joker than me. "Again about the chicken tits?"

Bob's dead eyes on me. Those of a sly demon. Striking. Piercing. Invading my soul. Not eyes at all. Tools. Keys.

"But as I said earlier, people also say chicken swells when you cook it," Bob continues. "The evidence: the meat rises due to the water that discharges into the pan."

"Discharges?" Will asks himself, having enough of his kin, giving Bob his back.

"The meat will also take up less space in the frying pan once cooking begins."

Will walks off.

I'm stunned as if tasered. He's not human, this guy.

"Both observations are correct and incorrect," says Bob.

I'm not one or the other, shrinking in size or getting

tougher as I'm cooked and aged. I'm aware of making a literal connection, but that's because I get it. Somehow, I understand what this cuckoo bird's saying.

"Remember the chicken breasts," Will says, thumbs up in the air and behind him like middle fingers.

"Sounds delicious," I say, masking my interest and, perhaps, gaining respect for Will's brother. But Bob's out of here before I can learn if this is true. Wesley whipping him back through the parking lot and out into the world. "Was he holding a pocket-sized copy of *The Art of War*?" I ask the silence.

About thirty feet from our goodbye, Will hoots, "Good riddance."

CHAPTER 25

Roshell
Paul (cousin)
~~Wretched (???) [don't remember]~~
~~Impatient (Golfer)~~
~~Bob~~

Metaphorically, the anesthesia has fully worn off. I'm completely awake. A born-again killer. A virgin murderer.

I'm a walking excuse to do bad things. So were Andy Warhol and Pee-Wee Herman. One in art. One in life.

I don't honestly know what the hell I am but glad I'm down to two people. I recognize the irony of crossing out the Impatient Golfer (a description that defines me) and ending all possibilities of partaking in that dumb sport again.

And Bob's left town.

Like a preschooler looking for trouble, I crumple the list and toss it. Just like the toddler I was. I'm prepared to reembody that nimble brat. Why the hell not? What have I got to lose by embracing my youth?

"You okay?"

"I'm asked that a lot lately," I say to Betty, watching my tone. "Come sit," I say out of character, playing the part, aware she's got something on her mind.

"Can we talk?" she asks.

See?

"Your memoirs." I don't sigh or lean back. I listen. Frozen. "I want you to have a chance to explain yourself. *It*."

"I'm an it?"

"No, bonehead," which doesn't come out as loving or demeaning but sad. Simply sad. And I still don't know what she means.

"It?"

Caringly, she says, "You're acting kind of strange."

"I'm not acting like anything. I just am."

We both tempt upturned lips. Neither of us commit.

"You know what I'm talking about."

"Yes," I say, "the memoirs thing. The stupid thing I wrote that's nothing. I sound like I'm talking about an affair, but it was nothing. Less than an affair. Obviously, that's the case. That it was less. But it meant far less than anything. Because I didn't mean any of it."

"Why write about...I'm not entirely sure what it was about, but if you didn't mean any of it, why write it? You know they were real thoughts. Don't lie to me."

"Of course, yeah, they were real thoughts. All thoughts are real. You have them."

"Okay. So?"

"Buttons on my underwear?"

"What?"

"Buttons on my dick. I don't mean you, Button, on my dick." I hold my head, something I don't do. "I don't want to get into that bullshit about my pet name for you again."

"You're not alluding to sex. Fine. Who cares, anyway? I just don't want to wonder so much."

"Okay. No jokes. No sex."

"Lance."

"Betty."

"Please. I'm not trying to make this difficult."

"Me either. But I also feel it's not important." I want to say that I was confused before. That I truly thought she was calling me an "it." She'll think I'm an old dimwit or teasing if I backtrack that much for something so inconsequential. "I don't want anything to be weird about it. What I wrote."

"Lance, talk. Just talk. I know you sometimes feel forgetful or slow."

"Goddamn it," I say. "I mean...see?"

"See what?" she asks.

Shit. "I'm not a dimwit," I say. "Or old."

"I didn't say you were either of those. I'm here to listen to how you feel."

"I'm forgetful sometimes."

"*That* I said."

"I've always been that way."

She pauses. I wait.

"It seems more often," she says. "Or you getting sidetracked is, maybe, more apparent lately."

"Maybe."

"So is that part of why you wrote that–those words? Or where it came from? I hardly remember what it said now, because I think I was in shock when I read it."

"I don't remember any of it. It was like a thought experiment. Just writing. Throwing out the junk in my brain. You know me. I don't write often apart from filling out newspaper crosswords."

"You hardly do *that*."

"I hardly do that. See?"

"Okay, but...an experiment is to test something out. So, are you testing your limits or something?"

"Sure. Just to see who I am. And I've done a lot of other things. To stay active and alive. But what am I supposed to do? I can't jog anymore. And I don't want to start popping pills. I've cut down on drinking. For you. Considerably." She doesn't get it. She should agree there. "It wasn't like I was talking about cannibalism or what I keep hearing is, uh, toxic whatchamacallit."

"Masculinity."

"Yeah, that."

"Like you explaining how rape used to be a fantasy for women."

"That's toxic?"

"It's a miscommunicated idea."

And here is where she proves she's as kooky as I. She's got a smirk pulling at the edge of her lips. She enjoys the rape debates. Or maybe the memory of our first rape discussion. The way we clicked and click. Knowing there's pain with love, even if it has nothing to do with actual rape. We're two crazies who are crazy about love. And I'm aware our connection has nothing to do with violating a woman through violent anger. Never has this been the theme. It's unbelievable, but the word "rape" had a different, less serious connation during the 60's and 70's. Watch any movie from that period, and you'll learn how rape references weren't made to bring attention to the atrocious act but are more comparable to the 1990's mild controversy revolved around wild girls flashing their tits to video cameras or S&M in today's erotica novels.

I say, "I don't feel...there's much to talk about."

"Wasn't there some nickname in there, too?"

"In where?"

"Your writings. *The Man Memoirs*. You had an alias."

"I think so." I can't say I don't remember. I wish *she'd* remember the name. Read my mind like she used to.

"What was the point of having a nickname? Were you wanting to be noticed but not found out? Or caught? Like the next Unabomber? Or were you experimenting with the whole idea?"

"I really don't feel like it was a big deal."

She's quiet. Is she convinced? Am I? Can one go through a want-to-kill phase?

"As long as you know that you can talk to me, Lance," she says. "No matter how strange your thoughts are."

"Yes, I know." Only, you can't go to your wife with this type of shit. "I appreciate it."

"Okay."

"Hey," I say, maybe over the top, "we should invite Roshell over for dinner."

CHAPTER 26

When I get mad, outraged, where my frustration tolerance with being out of control gets out of control, I crave blood and want to inflict pain. I've taken a vengeance pill. A shot of anger adrenaline. A quick-drip of boiled oil. Nothing intravenously, but a dirty needle straight to the back of my skull, leaving me speechless. The much-needed release of energy is more like flipping a switch than a buildup. I don't black out; I'm blank. And there's a highly-infuriated, point-blank scope that peers back and into myself, mirror or no mirror. I want to kill and end all things. Really, really wanting to end it all for everyone.

The only notion that could pull my head out of this swirling irritation toilet and into proactive fan-hitting shit is a full-blown scene of me planning out a kill in the movie *Roshell, Sweet Roshell*. A one-act play would also do.

As long as God doesn't damn the whole production before it gets going.

"Holy shit," says Betty to me, halting in the doorway at full military attention. "You're not kiddin'."

"About getting dolled up? I told you. I wasn't blowing smoke up your ass." I finish my tie. Turn from our reflection to her physical presence. "But I'm feeling frisky, so I might be doing something else to that ass later on."

"Shut up," she says, but meets me where I am in my head and in the center of the bedroom, allowing me to wrap my slithery dress-shirt appendages around her torso. "Do you have a thing for Roshell?"

"Don't be crude," I say, releasing her, holding onto playacting.

"Ha!" because she gets my choreography and dry delivery.

We're a couple of performers in a nutty theatrical production. Two goofs awaiting the arrival of the dinner guest, Roshell. The ideal victim. The hoity-toity know-it-all whose time has come. Unaware of what she's getting herself into, always vital for the audience's suspense. And the genius of the show is that one of the main players (Betty) isn't aware of how strange the night will be. Only Lance knows.

Only Lance Knows. I could see that on a poster as a title or quote. Written in red cursive. Below that: "A tragic comedy."

Imagining the tale of the dinner before greeting or eating or murdering is presumptuous and unprofessional. The audience is still getting comfortable. I need to stay focused. Let the scene develop. All asses in the house need to settle.

Should I do a mental checklist? Take a piss, wash my hands, and say "check" out loud to make sure I've covered all possibilities? That's not possible, is it? To control all of what can happen? I mean, I'm not actually directing a stage show here.

"Lance!" hollers Betty. I pause before entering the bathroom, face sopping with patches of agony, dreading the difficulty of pulling my dick out of these dress pants—the fancy shirt pushed down and covering the little guy like a pre-peepshow curtain.

"Huh?"

"You're not going to actually apologize, are you? To Roshell?"

"What do you mean?"

"Don't. Don't say you're sorry. Just have a nice night with her and me and maybe hint that you could be kinder. Or don't even say that. You two are different people who don't necessarily get along, and that's fine."

"Am I saying *that* nonsense?"

"I don't care what you say."

"You do."

"I'm not telling you what to say."

"Good."

"Let's have a pleasant evening and not make it weird. Don't get mean. Be kind."

"Got it. Can I drain my dang vein now?"

"I'm not stopping you."

"I was walking into the bathroom and stopped to hear what you were saying."

"I didn't stop you."

We look at each other. Weeks ago, I think I was an ass to Betty. I don't need to be that guy all the time. I appreciate her. Right now. What she's saying, how she's saying it. I don't need an epiphany to go back and right my wrongs or change or remind myself that I don't want another woman. I often have thoughts to telephone Betty to tell her how much I admire her. Because I really do. I might not make the call, but it's the thought that counts.

"I might shit, too."

She laughs, because she knows I purposely dumped on the connection we just had before dumping in the bowl.

I struggle with fishing the fat worm out from its zipper cave when Betty hollers, "Be nice," through the door. That wasn't necessary, and I stay silent. Remembering, telling myself, to be kind to our guest. Be pleasant. A host. It's gonna be a bitch to have that kind of restraint once Roshell from Hell arrives, but I can do it.

"Yes, dear."

When Roshell does enter the scene, it's too fast. I'm unprepared. I didn't do a checklist. I didn't talk out loud. I didn't shit. All I have is a burned image of my dopey face in the reflection. A blank, numb, old face.

"Don't sneer," I whisper, exiting the bathroom, joining

the ladies in my getup. Arms open, I say "Welcome."

"Hello," is Roshell's non-eye-contact greeting.

"Let's have a nice night," I say, arms still spread out.

She raises her eyes and fully takes me in, torso to shoes.

"Lance. You look spiffy."

"I was bored."

Betty fires a look of warning my way. Not a ton of concern in it.

"So," I say. "I had the idea to have an evening with two ladies. For company and whatever the night may bring us."

"I hope you weren't betting on a threesome, dingdong," says Betty, standing to hug Roshell.

I take a seat and smack Betty's ass. Roshell doesn't approve. I like it, though, when Betty breaks her own rules. Or does politeness not fit with Betty's definition of kindness?

"I thought: a game?" I say.

"Why not," says Roshell. She could've used another take. More rehearsal. Unconvincing. Flat.

"Lance has hors d'oeuvres, too."

"Really?"

"Store bought," I say. "But not cheap."

"You're not cheap."

"Thanks, love."

"I'm starving," blurts out the creature. "I'll take some whores doove rays."

"Whores doove rays it is."

Roshell is being funny. Showing us she can play along. For a while, anyway.

I'm thinking of that wacky theatrical-production-turned-movie starring Elizabeth Taylor. When she was older. Screaming at her real-life husband. *Who's Afraid of Virginia Woolf?*, right?

I rise to the occasion, ready to get this show going and the party started. I press play on the CD I cued up earlier today, preplanning like a psycho. The tunes are classical.

A mix of artists. Something I haven't listened to since the day I bought the disc at a garage sale fifteen, twenty years ago.

"What's this?" asks Betty.

"Some classy classical."

The music is louder than I expected and obnoxiously upbeat. Which means it will only get worse, these CD compilations usually beginning with their best non-copyrighted, royalty-free stuff. However it is that that business works.

I'm already in the kitchen and don't plan on returning to the living room to turn down the mess of horns and drums.

"How long are we going to listen to this?" Betty laughs. I do, too. The cutie.

"Click it off!" I shout over the lovely racket. "Put on some Bing or some-thing."

I can hear them whispering. Somehow, over time, whispering has fallen under the category of respectful manners among guests. Partaking in secrets, however, creates opportunity for brilliant mutiny. I can't let anyone but myself steer the ship.

"Roshell," whispers Betty, "we could find a playlist on the Internet. What do you like?"

"Country."

"Oh shit," Betty slips, loudly. They both laugh.

To prevent a revolt or loss of control, I make my eavesdropping known and say, "We might, or I might, have some Willie Nelson! Before he got twangy."

"You do?"

"I don't know."

"I don't think you do."

"Then, I don't. Shit."

Roshell probably couldn't tell by my tone through the door, but I'm pretty sure I briefly lost my cool. I'm future thinking again. How I'm going to get the powder in their mugs. How I'm going to get them to want tea. How far that offering is from now. How I need one person zonked out before the other goes down. The plan doesn't seem like it should make sense to me, and I'm not sure that it does or doesn't.

I hear Betty heading toward the kitchen from behind me. "They're in the oven, right?" I ask, losing and finding my bearings at the same time. "Keeping warm?"

"What are you doing?" Betty's come around the corner, poking her face into the kitchen like Costello.

"Me?"

"Yes." She fully enters. I'm standing with my arms at my sides. "What the hell are you doing in here if you haven't gotten them out?"

"Nothing."

"Nothing?" She laughs. I don't. "You okay?"

"Fucked shit, am I smiling again?"

"No. You look pale."

"I'm okay. I wasn't sure if they were done."

"They've *been* done," she says, a babysitter doing her best. "They're keeping warm. Here, I'll get the whore doovers, or whatever she called them, and you go in there so as not to keep our guest waiting." A filler line. But with purpose. I respect that. She's keeping it light while appreciating my efforts. And a decent improvisation. "You're bound to pull the pan out with your bare hands."

"I have human hands," I say, getting my wits back, clutching onto them for dear life. "Hey, you hear that one?" I shout as boisterously as possible when entering the living room.

"No."

"Aw, well. You missed it, then, didn't ya? A real knee slapper. So you like Willie?"

"What?"

"Nelson." I look through our sideboard of CDs. "Did you think I meant penis?"

"Lance!" from the kitchen.

"What?"

"At least be funny," Betty says off stage, staying in character.

I smirk, really loving Betty tonight, not wanting to put her down like a bad dog while, too, recognizing she's not a bitch. I don't think I'd ever think of her as a bitch as in a nasty, selfish woman who constantly barks back at the horny alpha. On the other hand, I'm committed to carry out the plan, and Betty has to be taken out of the picture I have in my head.

"You two," Roshell says, shaking her head, dismissing our humor, interrupting my thoughts. "I'm good with Nelson. Or Cline. Patsy."

"Who the hell is Cline Patsy?"

"That was slightly better," Betty says, entering with the snacks like Felix in *The Odd Couple*. "But not terribly funny. Did you know Lance is a professional comic now?"

"What does that mean?" Roshell asks me.

"Who knows? I should have Betty committed."

"Tell her about your stand-up."

"Sometimes I do it sitting down."

Roshell goes, "Hmm," which might be a pity laugh or shrugging off any possible acknowledgment. I can't tell, and I don't care.

"How are you with modern music?" I ask Roshell, keeping my back and ass to her, all the while, shuffling through the plastic squares of musical discs at an insufferable decibel level.

"I like some. Pop music."

"Lance has been working at a record store, too, you know. Vinyl never dying. Although, he still has his CDs."

"Am I being profiled?" I ask Betty, to which she presents a look of absolute confusion. I feel bad. "I'm sorry." And I am.

She accepts by squeezing the hand I give her and says, "We're just talking."

I swirl back to the CD collection and say, "Pop music, huh."

"Yeah," Roshell says. "Whatever that stands for. Popular music, I guess."

"You know," I say to Roshell, because an arrogant demeanor is key to riling her, "they call it soda music in other states." Betty gives me a look. "Thoughts, Betty Butt?"

Roshell chokes, swallows, and says, "Lance, I thought you were done with that nickname."

See? Roshell's a bitch.

"I'm not sure, yet." And I keep going, somehow, she now winding me up.

Careful. Be careful.

I ask the room: "Do you think people were more polite in the olden days?"

"Absolutely," Roshell jumps. "I can't believe how manners have gone away."

Betty doesn't respond. She knows I'm toying with Roshell, playing her like a melody. Or a cowbell.

I proceed, acting like the superior home-owning man with the pipe at the fireplace, so in character that my concentration bounces from direct attacks to foolhardiness without a hitch: "I wonder, though, if politeness, manners as you say"—Betty rolls her eyes—"is a branch of oppression."

"A branch?" Betty buts in. "Lance, just shut up."

"Seriously," I continue, wondering if people of my generation sound out of place when using "seriously" as an emphatic intro. "Black people saying 'sir' to police officers or people of authority. Raised that way. Since slavery. Women speaking out of turn. Men saying to 'stand back.'"

"Well, I don't agree with that," says Roshell.

"Sure. But maybe 'pardon,' and 'after you,' and 'I'm sorry' are all no different than 'yes, ma'am,' or 'ladies first.' Is holding up standards of politeness currently a white-person flaw?"

I see it in Betty's eyes. She appreciates my knowledge. She likes when I'm serious, because it's not often. I have a brain. I have feelings. I care about stuff. I can be articulate.

I think she's turned on. I wink. She sticks her tongue out like a brat. I'll show her what to do with that tongue.

"I don't know," says Roshell, disinterested.

"Well, maybe politeness is a thing of the past and you don't know how to deal with the change. I'm just joking. Kind of. Because none of us know how to deal with the future. We're all faking it or are a bunch of fakes. Like that little shit from *Catcher in the Rye* says. So I'm told."

Roshell has been put in her place minus my usual asshole-istic ways. At least I think I was conversational. I think Betty would agree, too. I like how I put that spin on the end, giving myself an advantage by making myself sound dumb about the Salinger book. And, truthfully, I am a little dumb about it. Because I don't remember if I read part of the story, the whole thing, or any of it. It was assigned in school, I'm pretty sure. Loudmouths and their cousins, quiet know-it-alls, love to bring up that book and its recluse author. I, personally, don't remember anything about it. I have a lot of memories like that. Ones I don't recall. Sometimes you talk so much about one thing, over decades, you're no longer sure if you've experienced the thing yourself. Like Bruce Lee quotes or James Dean's rise to stardom. I was alive during that time, but there's so much goddamn postmortem media surrounding them nowadays, you get confused.

Am I a loudmouth for referencing the book? Hope so.

"How's the hip?" Roshell guns at me. It's a cheap shot.

"Great," I pop back. "Healing time is remarkable. They weren't lying. How's the grub?"

Sensing the tension in the room, Betty says, "Dinner will be in less than an hour. Is that fine?"

"Oh, yes," says Roshell. "Terrific."

I'm going to go ahead and name what's lurking in the room: "Betty, are you sensing some hostility?"

"I'm fine," says Roshell.

Betty is watching me, eyeballing me, and allows me the next move.

"I'm fine, too," Betty says. "You?"

"I'm fantastic," I say, thrilled by the hunt.

We go on like this for a while. No board game, yet. Teeter-tottering conversations.

Betty's fairly exact with her internal cooking timer without checking it, and dinner's ready forty-five minutes later. Any nervousness or self-doubt has skipped on along with the banter beginnings I've been offering. My ability to quietly listen to the ladies is undeniable. But I also know myself, and that means I'm getting an urge. No longer wanting to sit still.

So I quietly consider outcomes. The big one being that I get caught. Evaluating how guilty I'll look after tonight's events if something goes wrong. If I have a heart attack during—Betty passed out from sleeping pills and Roshell dead—it'll appear as if I'd planned to kill the both of them. They'll raid the closet and everywhere else. The computer's online history. Knife sharpener in the dishwasher. They'd find my movie list with the underlined words. My kill list. My manifesto/memoirs. Rumors and truths will spread. It'll come out how I used to give candy to kids back when I was a kid myself. A thirteen-year-old looking for purpose. Wanting to be a teacher, not a perv. Those adult years I played at the park with my friend's kid and that kid's friends, because my friend's dad's other kid was having softball games at the other end of the block. That was me, dearly holding onto youth and not munchkin forearms; but try explaining it to a jury. In my 50's, I used to ride that rackety bike in the neighborhood, back when I first felt like the cranky old man on the corner bench. Or what about when I felt like the dirty old man peeping in on people's lives, something I admittedly and occasionally did during walks, as anyone would at any age? How I used to turn off the lobby lights at the car dealership without permission. I'd get headaches from the fluorescents. In hindsight, my reaction to those migraines made me seem clinically crazy. I'd also turn off the lights whenever I came into the office of that JD Home Improvement. I'd ask the secretary there to massage my shoulders. Snuffing out brightness became a signal that I needed a rubdown. First thing in the morning or after a long day. I thought it was funny and never made a move on the boss's sixteen-year-old niece. I wouldn't have wanted to. She was developed beyond her years, but I was thirty. And then there's my short story about a father killing his entire family and six pussycats—based on my great aunt and her piss-reeked/wreaked home (the murder part was fictitious). I still have that stored away somewhere. Would my high school still have records of my homework? That paper I wrote: "I'd Love to Kill, Please." My experiments with chat rooms and texting when they first came about. Roleplaying and sounding sadistic and, every once in a great while, acting as the weaker sex, the people at the other end taking my performance to mean whatever they wanted it to mean. When I was busted masturbating those (three?) times. Would those folks be subpoenaed? Make me out to be an indecent, sex criminal? Or, I guess, a fiend before found guilty? My high school pranks. The pedophile coach advancing but not scoring with me. The jokes about gays in high school. My recent stage time. Dabbling into dirty jokes and strip clubs in my late-twenties and again in my late-forties. Dipping in the dating waters at baseball games in my fifties. When I turned sixty, I flirted with every age over eighteen, quietly threatening to father the entire neighborhood. I still don't know why. And all the rest of my unusual and perverted, yet circumstantial, history to fit a profile.

But do I care?

I stir the prepared sleeping-pill powder into Betty's mug of steaming tea and watch the swirls, knowing I am a protector and how keeping her out of the design is vital. I wanted more of a motive for myself. But oh well. I wish Roshell was more of an inconvenience. A model for death.

A waste of life. But she's not that horrible tonight. Maybe this is the Roshell with whom Betty hangs.

I mean, I'm not beginning to go blind, am I? God, I hope I'm not accepting Roshell unconditionally.

"Am I getting that game?"

"What game?" Betty asks, finally suspicious of my antics.

"Uh...Yahtzee?"

"Yahtzee? What the heck, Lance?"

"Oooo, I haven't played in years," Roshell says, excited and pleasantly satisfied with the opportunity to display her first full smile of the evening. "Really, *years*."

"That settles it."

"Do we have it?"

"*I* have it," I correct Betty.

"What's with all of this ownership talk?" Betty asks. "Fine, it's your game. I'm not trying to move in."

We all snicker. Every one of us from a different perspective.

"I'm sorry," I say.

"And you don't need to apologize," says Betty. "You're just a friggin' weirdo tonight."

I retrieve the game. It's under the bed. Ready.

"I told you the other day, Betty, about the IEPs," Roshell's saying as I return.

"What is that again?" Betty asks.

"School accommodations," Roshell answers.

Betty's still unclear. I don't understand either and am not interested. But Roshell's running her lines anyway. An entire monologue is coming, I can tell. I'll set up the game so my character doesn't awkwardly stand with his hands in his pockets, the audience waiting for him to do something.

"And accommodating for whom?" Roshell asks herself. "I'll tell you what. Working at a school isn't the most difficult job, but it's the worst and least rewarding when the kids and the parents don't give a crap. You know

I retired, right? So much paperwork, IEP after IEP, until I'd finally had enough. A lot of students need them, but oh my god. And I come out of retirement for what? For *this*? I'm helping an alternative school," she tells me. We make eye contact a second time. I hand her the tea. I hand Betty her sleepy cocktail, unbeknownst to her. "And these kids. Let me tell ya." What the hell is she talking about? I must not have gotten the rewrites for this scene.

"Alternative school?" Betty attempts to determine or confirm or ask. She's filling the space before silence begins. Keep everyone engaged.

"An alternative high school. Yes."

"I don't know what that is," I say.

"High school?" Not funny, Roshell. "It's the *alternative* to the city high school." What a cunt. "So, being there with all of these, I'm sorry, dropouts, burn-outs, what-have-you-outs. I'm doing nothing but regretting my choice to be there." So are they. "All day long." Fucking torture for those kids. "Which isn't good for anyone." So quit and quit bitching. "And you wouldn't believe how much work goes into these IEPs."

"What's your title again?" Betty, being genial as hell.

"Teacher consultant."

"I don't know what that is," I repeat.

"It's not worth it."

"Worth going into?"

"What's not worth it," continues Roshell like cancer, "is the little Mexican kid who doesn't come to school. And I'm not being racist. He's a certain kind of kid. You'd know his type if you saw him. And his family. He's the only Mexican student there, but that's not my concern."

"This is about your ego," I say.

"And then that smile," Betty says, pointing at my jaw.

Dead silence until Betty sips, sips, and sips. She ends up finishing her tea. She'll be asleep soon.

I feel guilty. I get hot, as if I chugged the mug drug myself. I'm worried I put too much sleepy-time medicine in Betty's drink. Isn't her age a factor for the dosage?

Shit.

Roshell looks to Betty, ready to adlib some bad lines.

"I mean," I'm losing my thought. My words. Roshell has to be stopped, is all. She's not a decent person. More than a downer. She's terrible. I'm saying, "Our egos are everything. I'm not talking about the work you do with INPs...You're recognizing that your work might not mean anything. To anyone. That's your ego that's making you feel like you're not respected or valued."

"I don't feel disrespected."

"You still did the work," I interrupt back. *I'm* in the spotlight. "You were still obligated by the government to do your job. You still got paid. And your ego is making you think the work you're putting in should mean more, or else it's nothing for nothing. So you're attacking the Mexican family who doesn't concentrate on their kid, in a mostly all-white school. Isn't that what you've told us before?"

"That shouldn't matter."

"That they're all white? Of course it does. Don't be stupid." Oops. But go, go. "I feel super out of place when I go somewhere and find out it's a cookout with all black people. Or when a bunch of Arabic people are standing behind a counter at a gas station. They're just not my people. Not the ones I grew up with or know a lot about. But what you're talking about isn't coming from ignorance or being uncomfortable but that race-profiling babble. Not that that's not a real thing, but—or maybe race has nothing to do with it, but your ego sure as shit does."

Betty can't believe I'm delivering in this fashion, but it's the character's turnaround. His pre-monologue (prologue?) before killing. Betty looks tired, so I won't wink or say anything to my lovely, dreamy-eyed wife about having the situation under control.

Betty burps, too. Love it.

"Dinner was good, wasn't it?" Roshell asks us.

I shake the dice in the game's provided, imitation-velvet cup.

"You haven't played in years, you said?" Uh-oh. Doesn't look like Roshell's up for friendly conversation. I'll try again. "Remember the actress from *The Waltons*? When she was nude in *Playboy*? People were in such an uproar, it seemed like the world was going to end."

Roshell frowns. Betty quietly, and I believe sleepily, says, "I remember that."

"How times have changed," I say.

Betty, eyes closed, says, "Like Vanessa Williams or the girl who played the daughter in the Cosby show."

Roshell doesn't get it (us).

"Clinton," I say, rather loudly. "The scandal. Or Pamela's sex tape. A totally different time than *The Waltons*. Porn made public. And public happy."

Roshell clears her throat, not wanting to understand.

I say, "People get famous for having sex tapes. Supposedly leaked videos. So what's next, popularized and constitutionally-protected murder snuff films to add to YouTube terrorist videos?"

"I don't think I follow."

Actually, neither do I. "I think," I roll a full house, first roll, "I'm talking about experiences. Witnessing them. Being there when things change." I roll another full house. "You see that?"

"I don't think Betty's going to play."

I roll again, testing how deep in sleep Betty may travel. "*The Blair Witch Project* hoax was an experience," Betty says, suddenly awake and with it. "Ever see it?"

Roshell shakes her head and drops a messy roll.

"Lance and I just watched it," says Betty. "McCarthyism was another kind of experience. Even though we were kids."

I ask Roshell, a dart to the throat, "Were you born at that time?" She doesn't want to answer. I believe she's in her early sixties.

"John Lennon in bed for two weeks was an experience," Betty contributes some more. I think she's helping me, squatting in my corner, trying to keep the conversation alive and her eyes open. She's tired, and this is a face she's putting on. I appreciate it.

I say, "Experience is everything. JFK, 9/11, Woodstock. We lived through all of that. Blackouts. Wars." Out loud but to myself, I say, "Was I in New York when their big blackout happened?" I look up. Roshell's thumbing the scoresheets. "People are different than they used to be." I hand Roshell the dice cup. She rolls, not knowing where the director is going with this improvisational scene or why he's allowing it to play out for so long.

Whispering, wishing Betty a soft descent, relishing the thought of Roshell's neck fat between my fingers, I say, "It's the Christian bitches–Critches–that are bad. Not all old people. Not all religious folk or any one side to politics. Not all women. Not all young people. But people like you, Roshell." The first time I've ever uttered her name to her stupid face.

"I'm not Christian," she says.

Betty, like a drunkard, says, "Lance, are you defending upcoming generations? Because you never do that." She peeps at Roshell, no longer caring about presentation, lying her head down. Eyes closed, she says, "He doesn't do that. Defend people. The people of Earth? No. Zero earthlings receive Lance's camaraderie." She smiles at what might be a joke.

"Betty?" Roshell says. Does she see the desire in my eyes? Her face has changed shape like a supernatural villain. "Betty?"

"She's asleep," I say, deadpan.

"Why?"

What the hell kind of question is that? Or is it valid? This is a shocking moment, the seconds before you die, knowing you're going to die. That must be shocking to every person who's aware of his/her own end.

"Betty!"

Betty stirs. I raise my voice, too. "Betty! You playing?!"

Roshell jumps, startled, fearful of the aggressor. I'm already a threat. How neat. I haven't even attacked yet.

Betty, though, is out cold. I can tell. She wouldn't wake if I killed her friend here.

"Listen, sweetheart," she says to Betty, setting down her undrunk tea, eyeing it a second too long. "I'm gonna get going."

I say, "Okay. Thanks for coming over." I'm saying goodbye? How do I keep her here? I've said all of those things, but nothing incriminating or relationship-ending. I'm going to see her tomorrow? Or sometime this week?

She's leaving! The Getaway Terminal! A Lance Sendoff!

Should I stop her?

I don't.

And she's left.

You did not kill Roshell, Lance.

Yes, Betty is asleep. Peaceful as a hibernator. And here you sit. Sitting. You didn't even bother to stand when Roshell exited. And now you're contemplating over Hitchcock movies like *Rope*, wondering how the murderers kept their party guests/spectators attentive for the length of an entire party. Comparing your own production. How your character did nothing. How your end scene involved a board game, tea, and the wrong background music. No rope. No way to blockade. You lectured about some unhip nonsense and never physically approached the bait. And if you were going to do anything remotely devious, you left the gloves in the nightstand upstairs.

Draw the goddamn curtain, man. Fade the lights. This show's done.

"Betty? Can you hear me?"

CHAPTER 27

Awaking, sighing, immediately thinking, conscious as hell, beginning a new day, keeping my eyelids sealed.

What a fucking disappointment. Yesterday. Today. Moment after moment. Me.

Goddamn, fucking disappointing.

Is Betty alive? Did I kill her?

I open my eyes to take in the light and full capacity of my brain power.

Her eyes are exposed, too, staring at the ceiling. I remember that I assisted her into the bed from the living-room couch around 2 a.m. I, somehow, manage to lie still. In shock, probably. Staring at her staring.

She blinks. Turns her head toward me. Appears refreshed.

She asks, "What happened last night?" and snuggles, the distraction and warmth of her body stirs my blood and, if you can believe it, we have extremely passionate sex. Our mouths meet. Our bodies are slow. Our mysterious night must have awoken something primal. Our lives, the only ones we have. And we really do fit together nicely.

Afterwards, watching the morning sun warm our neighbor's white fence from our bed, I'm thinking I want more time. The day. The week. Almost like I'm wishing for an extension for yesterday. How the hell does that make sense?

For a moment, I recoil and really enter that space where you're trapped in a thought. An ice fossil. But I'm able to break out of the frozen-in-time feeling by saying,

"We should go see a show. A play. At a local high school if that's all there is around here. Or maybe check and see if something's on Broadway. New York."

She cuddles some more. And for the next few hours, the house is filled with brief conversations. Each room reaching its capacity. And then we're on to the next one. The entire day littered with self-subscribed and performed chores. The topic of taking a trip revisited over and over. Nowhere expensive. Nothing set in stone. A getaway.

A couple more hours pass, and I realize I'm in a fog. I state this to Betty. She tells me not to worry about Roshell leaving early. She'll talk to her.

More hours. I'm not sure if the women have spoken.

I've too easily written off Roshell. That's a confusing way to put it, seeing that I've removed her written name from a list, but it's accurate. She's no longer an option, has depreciated in value, and I'm having trouble envisioning how I'll handle future interactions with her.

I may also be shutting down. Briefly battling suicidal thoughts again. Overpowering them as fast as they come, dismissing the option as opposed to conjuring an end-all plan. Not much to overthink or get over in the first place. I'm so good at avoiding suicide, I could advise Paul what to do next time he thinks of dying by his own hand. Teach him how to stop being so goddamn stuck on it.

"I'm going to see Paul today. Or tomorrow."

"Good idea," Betty says, I swear, no surprise to her. How does she know which Paul I am referring to?

"My cousin," I say.

"I know." Her talent of reading my mind has returned. A sign we're swinging from the same vibe vine.

Thinking of that short list is strange, because it evolved (devolved?) from a long list of alive people. The long list is gone. But not the people on it.

And, now, the shortened list is gone. But not the people.

That's all well and good (whatever the hell that means), but I might have to face the fact that I'm not a killer. Am I? Not? I mean, shit, I haven't killed. So I'm not. Not yet.

Currently, I'm an average Joe without a sheet of paper, name, or target and having thoughts of offering my cousin Paul some—what are those called?—coping skills for his suicidal tendencies. In the back of my mind, if none of my words work, there are the thoughts of how to put him out of his misery. Last name on the list. Last man standing. Or would that be me?

I don't know anything about Paul, which is making me rehearse possible lines and outcomes and different delivery options during the drive to his place. By doing this, I've become self-assured that I'm not equipped. Unable to understand his emotions. I don't have the capability to inquire and can't ask him how he's doing, because I won't know what to do with his answer. I'm feeling worthless and frail, aren't I?

Instead of rapping with the sickly dog, I'm going to put it down. Gently whisper before pulling the trigger.

"What are you talking about, Lance?" I ask the empty passenger seat. *You don't have a gun.* "I don't want one," I say.

That fast, already inside, Paul's grabbing us drinks. Finishing his work-related phone call.

What kind of drinks? Pop? Beer? I've stopped drinking alcohol, pretty sure I'm growing out of it (the need for a buzz). More bored with the routine than the beverage itself. More lazy than determined to ride on the wagon. Because, come on, I can't be suddenly burned out at almost sixty years of drinking.

Set a goal for yourself. Paul's probably heard this from therapists before, but maybe coming from me will do the trick. I'll try out basic thought-provoking, talk-show jargon and he'll say, "Thanks, Lance." On a journey toward the best man he can be.

Or I could threaten him with the murder option first. *Stop moping, or I'll put one in ya.*

I know. No gun. So I'll have to stab the familial idiot with a steak knife.

I catch a glimpse of my puss in the glass of a framed photograph of him and someone else. Is that a guy? Is Paul gay? I might be locking eyes with Paul's dead boyfriend. Paul doesn't seem like a homosexual. What does that mean? I know some gays aren't flamboyant, but what's that mean? Do I care if he is or isn't? Do I care enough to try to understand what he's gone through? I think I could. If he's gay and wants to explain all of his gayness, I think I could listen. I think I'm understanding why calling someone a faggot, if they're truly a homo, is unkind.

But he's not gay. There's his life with his wife and that affair that cost him everything. That wasn't a beard or the first step to him coming out.

Man, he has unusual knickknacks. I've never seen anything like these. Maybe they're not unusual. For a guy his age...he's not that young. What is he, sixty? Is it unnatural for a single guy to have knickknacks, whether they're the common kind or not?

Look at this. He's into comic strips. Buying book collections of them. Character coffee mugs and framed drawings.

Are these rare items? Originals? Does Paul draw? Is he an artist? Over there is his military trinkets. Again, a reflection of my mangy mug in all that shine. Jesus, he's received a shitload of honors and awards. Does that say "Valor"? I don't know what I'm looking at. Medals as a pile of dirty laundry. Why is all of this in the dustiest corner of the living room? Actually, I believe this is a side room. Not a showroom. Not a spare room, but a place of memory with an old chair. A grandpa's rocking chair. An antique beneath a hundred years of embedded grime. Fuck me, is that *his* chair? I always picture Paul as being in his thirties because he was so much younger, playing by himself at family get-togethers.

What's upstairs?

"You look lost," Paul says. He's not holding glasses or cans.

"I do?"

"I don't come in here often. Probably going to store it all. Or maybe not. Trixie likes this room."

"You have a dog?" checking the floor for a shabby pillow or a basket of slobbery squeaky toys.

"No." He doesn't know if I've changed the conversation or what. "I thought you met."

I met? Met what?

"Maybe you didn't. And she won't be here until," he looks at his watch. "She'll be late."

I forgot he's a half-sentence smartass. Or maybe I'm feeling stupid.

I appreciate that he wears a watch. I'm not sure why I respect that.

"You want to sit?" he asks.

"Were you getting drinks?" I sound like a dick.

"I'm sorry. I had to finish that call."

"I'm not thirsty. I mean, it's okay. I'm okay."

"You sure?"

"Sure. I mean, yes. Sure I'm sure. I'm..." I stop. I don't know what the fuck I'm doing here. "I'm sorry if—I remember that you were getting married."

"Married. Am married."

"Right."

"No big deal. If you don't remember, I'm saying. It's no big deal. I wish I'd forget sometimes. I'm just joking."

Another one with twisted thoughts. I'm intrigued. Warped cruelty probably runs in our blood. Too bad he's about to lose all of his.

"Already?" I ask.

"Huh?"

"You're already wishing you'd forget that you're

married to Tracy?"

"Trixie."

I almost look for the dog again. "How long have you been married?" I ask as if conducting a job interview.

"Since, well, it was just before we went to your place. How long ago was that?"

"My place? Oh, the party thing. I wasn't really there. I was in my head, bracing myself for hip surgery at the time. I've had it swapped since then."

"Hip replacements must heal fast."

"It's outlasted your salad days, apparently."

He laughs at that.

Do I like Paul? What the hell's going on? I thought I didn't. I may have been thinking of someone else all these years. He's suicidal, though, right?

Seems I've gone from starring in a tragic something or other to a laugh riot.

"So, Lance, how have you been?"

"That's what I was going to ask you."

"Oh. I'm all right. I'm still, to be honest, a little confused as to what your message meant. I like that you stopped by, I just don't know—what do they say? What brings you to grace us with your presence?"

"Isn't there a 'pleasure' in that phrase?"

"Maybe from the other person," he says, winking. "The pleasure is all mine. No, that'd still be me. Not sure."

He has a tic, doesn't he? It's less dramatic or noticeable than it used to be. He was really hyper when he was younger. This whole situation is screaming stress in his ear.

"I was," I begin, "not bored, but I'm retired and trying to give back."

"You don't have to have a reason. Family is family."

"I can't be something else." I pause. "And I know we sometimes need people."

"Are you talking about me trying to kill myself?" Just like that. "I'm over that."

The tic subsides. He has a handle on it. Maybe all of it. It?

"That's great," I say, far louder than I planned to. "I know internalization is..." I only know the word. I have nothing else.

"Yeah. Can't complain. Trixie–not my dog–is good to me. She's a good person. A *person*." He smiles. So do I. "We had our problems early on, as I've spilled to you, but it's a second marriage. New marriage. Known each other a long time."

"Same here," I lie, not sure why.

"That's right," he remembers, creating untrue memories.

See? He's forgotten about me, too. Which means I'm an okay person for not remembering everything. And so is he. He's in good company. We both are. I bet he doesn't know Betty at all.

"Betty's a good woman."

Shit.

"What has it been, five years or so since you married?"

Double shit.

"Life," and he adds, "Tough sometimes."

"Yeah," I say. "Tough as titties. Hard, erect, raw, sore nipples." He's gone quiet. Maybe unaware of how I've turned the turn of phrase. I change directions. "You're ten years my junior, right?"

Paul is taken aback. Offended? "Something like that. Ten, twelve. I'm surprised you use that terminology."

"Hmm?"

"The word senior. Or elder."

"I didn't use *those* words."

Did I? I did. I implied the opposite of "junior." A fucking senior citizen. The two of us. A couple of elders. Seniors.

"I remember you always dismissing age," he says. "In general. I looked up to you because of that."

I appreciate this. I don't know what to say.

"We should talk more," I say. "Get together." I don't think I mean this.

"You golf?"

Is golf a man's sport, a filler sport, or a getting-older sport? (Or all of the above? Or none of the above?)

"I have golfed," I say, cheerlessly.

Moments later, I'm an ear. Someone to lean on. Here for my cousin. Suddenly available and close. We don't get too serious or sentimental. He never learns I came here to end his days. I, instead, discover that he's an alright guy.

Goddamn. That's goddamn corny, isn't it?

Goddamn it.

CHAPTER 28

I left Paul's feeling absolutely helpless. Or hopeless. A fraud. A wanderer. Confused. Unbalanced. Unfocused.

During the moped ride home, I rearranged the letters of L-E-F-T (as in leave) to F-E-L-T (as in feel). A less-than spectacular find that generated sadness.

Over and over, my words resound in my head. Old-men sports (golf) versus new-men activities (comedy, or "roasting," or online bullying). How Paul talked about YouTubers. How I admitted I fell out of the music world in my forties, in the 1990's, thirty years ago. I never took naps (didn't want them, didn't need them) until I reached a certain age (also around my forties), but cut that lethargy out by my fifties. But ever since I'd reached and passed my mid-sixties, I allow naps without guilt. Short nights, early mornings–no shame. Early nights and passing out from exhaustion–bothersome. This past year, fatigue is a sign of eternal feebleness.

To Paul, I vaguely addressed aging and currently recognize how insightful that was of me. At my age, to know I'm a stubborn bastard, is growth. (Even though I've known that for years.)

At home, to overlap the silence and thought-words I did and didn't exchange at Paul's, I say, "What do people want me to talk about? What do they expect of me?"

To reminisce? Admit to watching and listening to the *The Fred Allen Show*? Or the radio show *Suspense*? I won't, because I never knew about those until satellite radio. I don't know or remember what Fred Allen looks like or if he was ever on TV. I remember Paul Newman starting charity food in the 80's. *American Bandstand* in the afternoons, in the 50's, I think. I had a friend from elementary school who was on *The Howdy Doody Show*. I remember *77 Sunset Strip* when I was around eleven or twelve, I'm pretty sure. I was allowed to stay up for that. At family parties, maybe some people listened to radio programs, but there were no longer fireside chats for kids my age. We were past that by then.

Well, hold on. There were the baseball games I listened to with my grandpa in the late 1950's. That was a special time with the radio.

Somehow, I've gotten to images of those giant tube TVs that sat on the floor. The boob tubes. "The box." The time I spent in front of one particular television set with my girl Marilyn. When I was thirty-something. I briefly lived with her, she at my place. I was able to do that, pull that off, put up with cohabitation for just under two years. Maybe I was twenty-something. I always have trouble narrowing that time down. Anyway, she mentioned I should start wearing wrinkle cream. Apply it before bed. I asked her not to put her vain stuff on me. I spelled it out, explained I was being literal. Aging didn't concern me. At the time, and *only* around that time, I admit I was obsessed with checking my looks in the mirror. My physical changes were becoming apparent. Every week, something new. (Maybe I was forty-something.) Also, at this time, there was a song that used to get me really down.

Man, I felt somewhat psychotic when I was twenty-five, or twenty-six, or twenty-seven. Whenever that was. Probably all three of those years. Because I was obsessed with another woman named Michelle. There was this song that would get me so low. I can't remember the song title, but I was just as infatuated with the tune as I was with her. I haven't thought of or heard that song in years. Used to know the lyrics and melody like riding a bike. Something about having fun in the sun and the seasons going away.

Yes, Michelle played with my heart. Crushed it and my body surrounding it. Like Time. She wasn't able to communicate how she felt. Not properly or well enough where I could make sense of her words, her intentions, her love, her life. She had some personality disorder, for sure, thinking back on it. And meeting her had ruined my opinion of love for...ever. Up till now.

And so, she wasn't the one.

I'm feeling uncomfortable because I think I may have memory swapped the women's names. I think I lived with Michelle and was obsessed with Marilyn. No, that can't be. I didn't live with the person with whom I was obsessed. And that song was the center of that fixated passion. The Beatles' ode to obsession, "Michelle," had nothing to do with that time in my life. And M. Monroe definitely had nothing to do with any of it.

I know in my heart those two were more than names in my memory bank of today. The fixation on them has cursed my thinking. That's all.

I want to do the right thing. Do right by Betty. I can move straight through with that idea. It's an action I can get behind. Or in front of. And she deserves the rightness of it. Hell, so do I.

"Hey."

"Hey, Betty Butt," I say back. I didn't know she was home. How long have I been in the dark staring out the window?

"I haven't heard you call me that in a while."

"Maybe your ass is on my mind."

I should take pride in my playful pronouns. Don't be so hard on myself.

"You sound funny," she says and turns on the lamp. "Why are your eyes red?"

"They're not. Where were you?"

"Folding clothes in the basement. What's going on?"

"Nothing."

"Your eyes are puffy."

"They're not."

"How would you know?" She inspects my face. Shit. "Are you crying? Or did you spray yourself?"

"Spray myself?" I've accidentally confessed. She drops whatever she's holding and comes to me quick, a mommy kissing booboos.

"Lance, what's the matter?"

This is a nightmare. My thoughts were a nightmare, and now I've got to relive them. Tell them. Fully awake and super alert.

"I'm thinking."

"What about, sweetie?"

She's really, really concerned. That feels good. Didn't I get enough of that attention when I was a kid? Have I not received this kind of sympathetic worrying from others in a while? Betty's there for me, but could she be more present in my life? In my thoughts? In my head? I never needed that kind of gooey garbage growing up. I played football. I banged girls. I made fun of boring teachers. I held my head high with the best of them. I brushed off the suckers. I was strong. I *am* strong.

Wasn't I? Aren't I?

Generalizing those life events, putting them side by side like that, doesn't represent me. I'm more than the blonde, scumbag jock in the 80's movie.

"I'm thinking," I repeat.

"You said that."

"The leaves are pretty."

She leans back to scope me out. "Well, *that* doesn't sound like you."

"I like fall. You don't."

"I do. Fall's never been my favorite, but that could change. It could be. The leaves are pretty."

"While I was sitting here, even right now, I'm thinking..." Damn it, this is difficult. "When I was—I don't know, thirty-three, thirty-two. I was rude, probably too rude, to an old lady at a store. I'm thinking about that. And seasons changing. I'm thinking about that, too. Turning our clocks back." She's attentive. I haven't lost her. "When I was eighteen or...yeah, probably eighteen. I was rude to this little girl with an ice cream cone." I look at Betty and realize I'm waiting for her to scrutinize me. Wanting her to. She's not, but I'm aware of being defensive. I'm prepared to stand up for myself. Ready to argue, just like any other boy at recess. Just like Russell, who used to tease me about the cigarettes he'd leave behind whenever we did construction together. The smoke curling toward me, bothering me. And I was a grown man, then. I never liked Russell but acted like we were friends. He pretended, too. We were friendly. "How do others see me?" I ask Betty. And I'm bawling my goddamn eyes out. She's holding me and rocking me. I hate that I can be this weak. That I've been busted weeping. She's not saying anything. She's squeezing. That's nice. I haven't cried in fifteen years or so. Yeah, fifteen. I remember. "I haven't cried like this since the night before my sixtieth birthday."

"I've never seen you cry," she says.

"I'm sorry." I quickly wipe my nose—a bad, bad kid.

"No, I love it. I don't *love* it, but you understand."

"No," I say, flat. I don't understand. Am I being mean?

"You're not as bad of a person as you think you are."

I relate Betty's positive message to what Bob was saying when calling me a swelling and shrinking chicken, that we don't have one appearance but many kinds and different versions of change.

"I'm not crying anymore." I straighten my back. Fix my posture.

"It's okay."

"I'm not doing that." I stand.

"It's good to let that stuff go."

"What's inside is inside."

"Why leave it there? Let some of that out."

"No."

She blinks like I'm an owner-betraying mutt. I didn't raise my voice. Is she scared? Maybe she should be.

"Listen, Lance," she stands and holds my hands. I feel like a dork. "I'm sorry if I hurt your feelings."

"Huh?"

"I'm sorry for being on you when what you were doing was nothing but exploring life. Golf, the record store, being with younger people, stand-up comedy." She laughs. Not at me. "I came on too strong. I was confused, I suppose."

I'm making fists.

She says, "You're not a bad man. And I'm sorry I wasn't listening or respecting your needs."

Betty not listening was part of the reason I've been struggling with finding myself, my likes, my interests at my age, but she's not the reason I am who I am.

"It's not your fault," I say.

"Okay." She's confused. "*What's* not my fault?"

Her tone has intensified. Is she offended?

"Me crying," I lie, not explaining my need to make someone bleed.

"Okay, but I'm here for you. Even if you want to go back and try college again."

"I don't think so."

"That I'm here for you?"

"No. College."

"Okay. But I would support you."

"Thanks."

"And as far as I'm concerned, you've been minoring in a course on the quality of life anyway. At the ageless age of seventy-four."

Spoken like a true actress.

CHAPTER 29

The benefit of aging is passing down and carrying over knowledge.

On the other hand, is that theory worth anything for me in the long run? Because I won't be here for the long run. No one will. There is no existence in the long run. And I get that people's short runs make up the long life-distance relay race for humanity, but my experience is only worth something for me because I experience it for me. Isn't that right? Dad said experience is overrated. But whether I'm breathing Earth air later on or not, I'm a part of a chain reaction. Or the butterfly effect. So, I *am* a part of the long run, right?

Stupid stuff like witnessing the meaning of Roy Orbison's song "Ooby Dooby" change from dancing and boogying to weed smoking and watching my buddy Charles take his first hit off a doobie while singing the song is a perfect example of a solo experience. Or what about the kids in the 80's giggling at the "My Ding-A-Ling" rap song, no one telling them the innuendo at least had a toy reference the first time around (along with allegations and convictions of original songwriter Chuck Berry being a sex predator)? There's a gap of information there, and my involvement is more essential because of that gap. Since 1967, whenever I hear or say the word "afternoon," I immediately tap into my album-listening days and jump to each and every melody transformation of The Moody Blues' "The Afternoon: Forever Afternoon (Tuesday?) / (Evening) Time to Get Away" like it's my goddamn theme song (privately scolding everyone else for their attachment to Tuesday). Sitting here thinking of Lennon singing about wheels going round and round while simultaneously looking up Terry Jacks, the singer of that song "Seasons in the Sun." All of this, the crap I don't have to prove, is proof of being alive. Me from then and my memories today.

(Even though it's too late in the day to be on the computer—never a fan of the Internet—I come across some interesting and worthy music news from Canada about someone impersonating Terry Jacks. This imposter took advantage of women two decades after the one-hit-wonder did his thing. The tidbit is appealing, because it's appalling.)

I click off the computer, disregarding that tech guy's advice to always leave it on, and only put it to sleep. Because not to follow directions is to kill it.

With my finger still on the off button, I think about the evolution of acquiring information, and how personal information used to entail a goddamn telephone number, and how we've phased out operators and their switchboards.

Offering information was one of my talents at the record store. I gave life to what one doesn't and can't get when retroactively exploring. It's like stalking someone in a squeaky house. A map of the floorboards won't help. You have to watch, listen, and learn or else you'll expose yourself.

Young people, specifically teenagers, don't know anything. Old people, the wise, aren't much better. Maybe some old women know a thing or two. Because they paid attention while the men, now old bastards such as myself, were busy trying to figure out things in the moment, just to prove they would be right about those things at a later date. (Didn't I do that a moment ago, proving my value by looking up what I remember?) I'd say women figure out how to do things in the moment, even if they don't get what they want. There's a proactive history to back up that opinion.

I turn the computer back on, it taking long as a son of a bitch, and clear the history and cache as suggested by Wesley (and reiterated by Paul upon my visit). Erasing computer searches is for peace of mind, helps the mainframe guts work properly, and is not because I fear the FBI. In general, I don't think Internet surfing is good for the brain.

Not sure how to put the fucking thing to sleep, so I jab the off button one more time to put the both of us out of our misery. As long as the monitor's black, I'm satisfied.

And like that, another switch inside my head flicks on. Still sitting in the dark, Betty finishing her work so we can watch a spooky movie tonight. Somehow—the brain and the connections it makes, maybe from the sound of a hardly-audible crunched leaf outside—I remember being on my way to a Halloween party in my late twenties, looking at my blood-splashed face in the rearview mirror. How fake blood wasn't as real looking or easy to come by. How different it was back then. Using household items. Smelling of condiments half the time. How less frightening and gory. But I'd seen *The Texas Chainsaw Massacre* a couple years earlier, and there weren't yet video stores to rewatch and jog the memory. Movies had theatrical runs for a certain period of time or were rereleased months or years later. That *Massacre* movie, though, really piqued my interest. Only, I couldn't remember how the guy looked, the one the teens picked up in the van at the beginning. I had already carried a blade; "borrowed" a friend's mom's expensive black wig and someone else's dirty, hippie clothes; and added red paint specks to my forehead, cheeks, and mouth. I just wanted to be a crazy person. Looking into my own eyes as I drove to the party. Listening to Lesley Gore's "Sunshine, Lollipops, and Rainbows." Understanding the satirical power a song could possess before the ritual became widely popularized years later (a style originated by director Stanley Kubrick, I believe). It was a messed-up moment for me, that's for sure.

On another note, perhaps from one played in that TV commercial melody, splicing one thought with another, I'm wondering what happened to that Wretched fellow from the kill list. Was he a customer at the shop? What made him significant enough to write down? Because I came across a record number of shit-for-brains and dickheads there. The lack of finding who he was, but taking the time to scratch him off the list, is extremely disappointing. Like lost treasure. Lost needs. Grieving over the unknown. Wasted efforts. Forgotten memories.

About eight or ten years ago, before I met Betty, I cried over the whittled heart and the love-story obstacles in the movie *Magic*. Anthony Hopkins gives the psycho performance of his life. The guy (the character) doesn't know his purpose. He retaliates against life in the end. Fuck, times can be complicated.

Outside, several leaves crunch. This time, I notice in real time. The giant sun illuminates the ground, the day's finale' before all is black. And through the window, I make out the jogger. He must be adding a run this evening, possibly due to daylight savings. Possibly taking my advice, fitting in a second jog. I'm not going to make a big thing out of this. I don't need to make unnecessary connections about looking at the bright side of things. I wouldn't be able to figure out the subtext anyway. In a book, I'd flip through and catch a single paragraph detailing the jogger's thoughts: *After twenty minutes, I feel more alive. My aching knee and back-hunching go away. On cement or not. Physical therapist or not. I feel loose, mobile, and ready for life.*

My quicksand has hardened into a beach paddy. I need to get off this goddamn island.

"Butt!"

"What?!"

"You want to go out?"

"At this time? I thought we were watching a movie!"

"Come upstairs."

"In a minute. Are you okay?"

"Don't start asking me that. I won't be able to live the rest of my life with you asking me questions like that. Giving me a sappy look."

"So then, what, asshole?"

"That's better...uh...I'm thinking of going out for a drink."

Her basement silence is a poisonous fog, slowly wafting upstairs.

"Okay," she says, quieter.

"Is that all right?"

"Yes. Do what you have to. I'll probably fall asleep on the movie."

"Are you bummed?"

"No. I'm being honest."

"Come up."

"I don't want to go up and then down and then up again. I love you. I'll see you later. Tomorrow morning."

I come downstairs. I see her. She sees me. No big deal.

"I'll be back before light."

"That's funny."

CHAPTER 30

The last performance begins with kids. The little boy who's two or three (can't tell, having no history of aging siblings, stepchildren, nieces or nephews inside my home life, boo-fucking-hoo) seems boring. To have to babysit or, god forbid, raise a miniature man must be hell. Standing above the stumbling, gabbing tike must be the older brother. A wannabe adult—if not a young and creepy neighborhood ghoul—who's not really keeping an eye on the smaller one. He seems to have aspirations to take on, or take over, the world. It's in his stance. I'd guess he's around seventeen. Looks like a self-righteous punk, if you want the truth. Someone who's going to protest for five or six years about something he'll never again consider for the rest of his life. I wouldn't like him if I were his age. If in this instant, he were to magically sprout to a fully-developed man, I'd start a fistfight with him. The middle kid of this front-yard family is a girl. She seems to have her head on straight. Wise. Hates her street. She's too beautiful and has been shunned for the nine, ten, eleven years she's been beneath her father and his shadow. That's Dad over there, playing with the front door handle this entire time. He presents as an imbecile without effort. Is Mom not home?

I've never seen these people before now and, obviously, don't know a thing about them—their home and existence being outside my usual block-observation and daily-musing range.

As their granddad (a tolerable title), I'd be thinking

that I should've said more and done more and didn't. From the brood's perspective, I'd be a failing nuisance in need of diapers and assistance. I'd eventually burn down the home because of an unattended stove burner.

There must not have been any family to take care of the poor guy. Burnt to a crisp.

My family wasn't there when I needed them most. All that regret for nothing.

This family may suck, but I'm happy to never have started one of my own.

During the rest of my walk to the bar, I come across nothing else of interest. For about half a mile, I walk without enjoyment. Not feeling one way or the other about having nothing in need of my attention, either. This must be that neutral emotional state I hear so much about. Lovely.

I've been driving past this simple B-A-R sign and the place below it for the span of its survival. Probably fifty-some years. Never been inside. Never been this close.

I open the door to this seedy scene and again think of having targets, prey, potential kills. How fulfilling it would be to see someone and know what a bad person he is and end him. The blood spilled by movie psychos and real psychos, along with the music of my brain—all the melodies of sounds with which I've grown up—are marching under my skin, down from the roots of my head hair to my forearms, bringing sensations to my gums and original teeth. My heart is warm under my tongue. Beating and providing gas for the soul. I'm geared up. Ready to fight. The perfect thoughts when entering an unfamiliar bar, don't ya think? Because, in this moment, I don't need to think up a motive to kill. I'm ready.

The atmosphere of the place is predictable. Dark. Sticky. Cigarette stank in the walls. Beer stench sealing clean-air gaps. The typical glowing bar counter. Mirrors on every wall. Chrome rails guiding you nowhere. Bottles. Glasses. Red booths.

I bump into a wobbly table placed too close to the entrance. Four people sit at the bar counter. One of them loud. Two others thought they'd slipped into a secret joint for some fun fondling. (They'll never return to BAR nor explore another joint like it.) At the end of the rows of stools leans an extremely wrinkly lady, her light weight held up by one foot. Probably the owner. No waitress in sight. A bartender appears from below and won't look my way. I can't tell if it's a man or woman. Waitress, waiter, bartender, it doesn't matter. They usually don't notice me. Whether this is an epidemic, social problem, or the repeated result of bar employees avoiding my aging face, I don't know, but I haven't had a server of any kind pay attention to me for some time now.

I'm regretting coming in here. Why didn't I scooter to the café by the record store? Or take an insane walk with the new bionic hip? I should turn and exit, only, the pleasant aroma of burnt burger grease is a major enticement. Do I need the grill lard? No. So I should leave. And I plan to when I hear the word "birthday" followed by a single CLAP and then laughter from arrogant men and shitty women.

I fully step into the false night of this place and notice white, year-long Christmas lights along the top of one of the backroom walls. To Betty, I'll probably describe this corner as a dank banquet area. Because what else is it? What purpose does it serve? Why in a bar? Were there pool tables and a Pac-Man arcade back here at some point? Two booths here at the doorway. Another near a crane game in the corner. Beyond these is an open space taken up by covered, foldout tables.

If it weren't for the placement of the booths, how they obscure and blend what should be an abrupt entrance—me standing at the sidelines of no-man's land like this—I'd be unintentionally crashing their bash. I've also risen, standing at the top of a yard-long, inclined ramp connecting the two far-different sections of BAR (always appreciating side rooms that provide access and exit ramps).

I see *30!* stamped and stickered on the table and pitchers of beer, haunting the group from those half-a-dozen black balloons struggling to float away.

Still as a post, I'm definitive about something. I'm deciding–have decided–to kill my inner-self. The frustrated one. The guy without the motives. I'm too old to change but not too old to act. So I'm going to order some drinks. I'm going to make a poor decision tonight, to end the indecisiveness. Probably, I'm this exact and direct because my own birthday will be with us soon.

Just like that, after a few shots and a couple beers, mulling over the TV program without a single thought, I make it back toward the Celebration Room one last time. Because someone in there is fucking rude and ruining the festivities.

"Sorry, sorry," someone apologizes for Mr. Insensitive, a title Betty once gave me. The someone, a smoking-hot lady, isn't talking to me but projecting this general statement to excuse the ruckus that's polluting the place. Mostly for the new guests who've arrived after me. There's a specific person being addressed, I realize. Sitting by herself in the smaller booth by the crane game. "It's his birthday, and he's been drinking since this morning. It's a rough one. Thirty. I'm sorry about him."

"She knows it's a rough one," says the birthday man who's mastered standing and sitting at the same time. "You've probably had some rough ones, right?" To the alone woman, he's pulling this shit. "I got you, babe. I can tell, and it'll be all right. In the end. When you die. When *we* die."

He's making fun of the woman's age. Her life. Her looks, but her life. Her experiences. Right to her face.

"Alright, Garry, knock it off, birthday boy."

Yeah, Garry. Listen to your mom, or whoever she is.

I pay special attention to the booth woman's reaction so I can identify her as an outsider and not a sulking guest of the birthday party. And I'm right. Clearly, she's not with them. But I wish she were, for she needs protection.

Still leaning against the doorframe of the entrance to this banquet hell, I will Garry to gaze in my direction. He doesn't. Not yet.

"He's sorry."

"Sorry for what?" says Garry. "I didn't do anything. And I'm not drunk."

Honestly, he doesn't appear drunk.

"What's your name?" he asks the woman in the booth.

"Have a good night," she says, excusing herself from the room.

"Wait, wait. I'm not being rude. I'll buy you a drink."

"I had mine, thank you."

She'd leave faster, but her arm's tangled by her purse strap and coat. I want to help and walk toward her, rising in height a tad because of the ramp. At the top of the incline, I'm three inches taller. But she still doesn't notice me. Not yet.

"Are you–how old are you?"

"Stop, Garry!" says the apologetic woman, still sounding like a mother. But I think she's a sister or a friend. A good ten years older than him.

"It's my wish to know how old you are."

"Shhhhhh!"

"There's nothing wrong with asking how old she is," Garry stresses. I agree with him, not his approach. "I don't want to make an assumption. You want me to make an assumption?"

"I'm fifty-eight. Happy Birthday."

Good for her. Because her age should mean something to her and everyone around her.

But is she a nasty person? Maybe she's having a bad day. Or is an alcoholic. Was she eating? Is she here with anyone? Is she a regular?

She looks at me. Wants to leave. I'm in her way. I move, accidentally blocking her.

"Sorry," she says, but it's callous.

"You okay?" I ask.

She ignores me. Continues on. My concern deserves recognition. I'm pretty sure she's a bitch.

"Do you know her?" Garry asks me.

I turn away and watch Ms. Fifty-Eight not exit. She sits near a gambling machine. Orders another drink. Is an alcoholic. No, she's ordered a Coke. A diet. Is she waiting for someone?

I get one more beer and close my tab. Watch her dance. She's no longer sitting. Not boogying on the floor either. She adjusts her body, rubs out her sciatica, and sways to the softly-playing song. She doesn't sing. She's a tad overweight.

Her focus is not on the gambling game. She has an entire day she's trying to sort out. Probably the whole week. Needing to plan next week, too. And this Garry boob is distracting, yapping about her moves all night. Cougar calling. Slowly making his way into the bar of BAR. Wanting to schmooze with us more-mature folk.

He's with the last of his friends. The mom/sister hanging in there for her son/brother. Has to be a family member if not the designated driver. His life support.

Garry's loud words—still not drunk and more sober than he was when I first saw him forty, forty-five minutes ago—drip like venom from surface compliments. Encouraging Ms. Fifty-Eight, and women, and aging, and independent thought all while dancing like a jackass. He's terrible at faking positivity. Unless he's putting on an act, purposefully and pessimistically probing us all. Whenever the topic of past experiences arises, he says, "They know what I'm talking about," and seeks the older people in the room. Those who have surpassed him. Or pre-passed him. Slowly gathering that he's come to the wrong place. Because there's nothing here. Nothing he'd want. It's not a present-granting community. Nothing worth living for here at BAR.

Tonight, he was sure he'd be cared for. Only, Garry's buddy Freeze—saying the guy's name fifty goddamn times—never showed. And he isn't going to show. The man of the hour is nothing but a lonely, first-class bum.

But I don't care what he's groaning on about. He needs to cool it or shut it.

I switch my attention to Ms. Fifty-Eight. Lost in another tune, jamming. I've never heard the song before tonight. An older country ditty, I think. At least, it sounds older. Older than what? What the hell does that even mean?

"This is my jam!" hollers the birthday brat. The man brat. Brat-man. He's full of nonchalant insults rooted in impersonations designed to offend previous generations. Stupid phrases and home-grown lines delivered to no one. A butthead who can't help himself but imply and reference. Every day of the week. All hours of the day. He doesn't listen. He doesn't change. He doesn't care. He's in love with his own pathetic and shitty interests that feed his excessive ego and arrogant ignorance.

He stands and mirrors Ms. Fifty-Eight's groove. Even her angle. I'm immediately mortified for her. My stomach clawing at itself. Her ass lifts, one cheek at a time. Her arm rises like a cobra from a basket. Her elbow at rest on the back of the stool. Her one heel turns. A hair whip. All traits of the females of her era. I recognize the later version of the hippie shakes. Her age makes her a 70's girl in skin-tight jeans and not the miniskirt ones from the days of peace and love. I think birthday Brat-man is having some reflections of his own. Intentional, condescending bullshit shit. Ready to sink his expensive, corrected teeth into the soft tissue that is the vulnerable fat of her life.

She massages her own neck, perhaps, anticipating the throw-up words that will project from the Brat-man type. Because right after her kneading, he says, "You all right?" like an unethical doctor.

Jesus, I'd like to challenge this defecation to a push-up contest. Or an arm-wrestling match. Like the good old days. Civil, seated, goal-driven. Flex. Grip. Slam.

"Hey," I say. I think of saying, "back off," or "take it easy," or "birthday boy, show some respect," but I keep it simple. From the diaphragm, I say, "Shut up!"

He doesn't laugh or wave me off. He doesn't call me an old man. He continues to dance. To imitate. To mock what's before him and all those who came before him.

Stupid, silly me. With my outburst, heckling the heckler, I've accidentally gotten Ms. Fifty-Eight's attention. And now she realizes what Brat-man's been doing. It's my fault she blushes. Embarrassed far beyond any mistake she made as a cheerleader or at that track meet.

She's beat red in the face. Fucking purple.

"I said, 'Hey,'" I say. "Sit down, boy."

I sound like a racist southerner. Man, if this guy's Puerto Rican or half-black...I'm fumbling through principles and values I would have liked to pass on to younger people. What am I conveying here?

"Are you with her?" he asks.

"I could be." I don't know what the hell that means. I think there's a few possibilities. "Leave her alone."

"I'm not bothering her. You're being loud."

"*I'm* being loud?!" I yell. "Okay. No, sure. I'm loud right now."

"Fuck yeah you are, bro. Why don't you keep drinking your–"

"I said to shut up," I repeat, quietly. He stops talking. He's staring. He was being polite. I've ruined any possibility for peace. I've gotten physically closer, too.

"Leave it alone," he says.

"Shut up," like a heedless movie director.

Her purse is tangled again. On the stool, this time. Low, gripping the crosses of the lengthy chair's legs. She doesn't want to squat. Her knees hurt. She's been shiatsu-ing her one thigh all night.

"Listen, bro," says Brat-boy, downgrading himself,

coming toe to toe, sneering at Ms. Fifty-Eight struggling with her bag and its tentacles. He's ready to call her out or giggle, I know it.

He's not interested in me or our chat. But I'm waiting. For anything. Him to try another catcall or eyeball me. Any fucking thing.

But my stare, man. It summons his attention like black magic. He looks over his shoulder and up at me. Because I'm taller. And I wink just before kicking his shin. Like a professional UFC fighter or biker who's been through it all. I also connected my elbow with the top of his head. Both moves practically in sync.

He falls back a couple inches and reflexively pushes me, more out of instinct for protection than retaliation, and I lose all balance. The room's lifted, and I feel a whack at the side of my shoulder. A punch to my hip when I drop. The landing is hard, fast, and awkward and forces me to arch my body. The back of my head dings off metal and knocks a second time against more metal. I rest my cranium there.

No one crowds me. Brat-boy's holding his face, laughing off the incident. Because I'm older. Supposed to be scrawnier. Fragile. And I've fallen. In his mind, proving the theory.

Blood, though, is running down from his eyebrow. I split his forehead open with nothing but my power.

"You're bleeding," says a man.

I smile, nice and broad. Because someone from BAR caught my handy work. Recognizes what I've done. How I've managed to make another man bleed from a flat area of skin.

"You hear me?"

The man's leaning over me. Keeping his distance because we're strangers. But talking to me. Looking at me like a brittle brick that could be removed but should maybe stay where it's at. He's concerned for my wellbeing.

"That was a bad fall," says a woman.

I don't agree.

"He hit his head on the ramp."

"I think you hit the railing when you fell."

Those were the two smacks. No one else touched me. Just assembled handicap pieces retaliating for being unnoticed. Got in the way of a bar brawl.

Ms. Fifty-Eight sees me down here.

What are you going to say to me? I defended you.

"Ridiculous," and under her breath, on the way out with her stringy purse bag, she adds, "macho crap."

"We need more napkins. There's kind of a lot of blood."

I can't see the birthday man/boy. He's blocked by his friends who are talking him into calling it a night.

And I swear, Wretched is leaning against the jukebox. But this place doesn't have a jukebox. And I don't know what the hell Wretched looks like, who he is, against what or whom he fights, why he would matter right now. What he meant to me at that time in my life. For what values did he stand? Pride? On his own head?

I can see myself getting up, rejecting assistance. Reach the door. Exit with finality, even though I've got something else to say. And there's a lot of people here to whom I could say it. It's never too late.

Involuntarily, I reach back and touch my skull to see what's going on behind the ears. Seems to be washed in sticky blood. Not too much, I don't think. There should be enough in me to keep going, keep thinking.

I'm doing all right. At the moment. On my own. Building myself up as I lay sprawled out on the tacky floor, at the center of the ramp for the disabled. Ironic, seeing as the incline incapacitated a fit and fighting man such as myself.

The fallen hero. Against them all. If that's a hero, then that's me. Making my way, the journey, up my own slope. Dodging myself and hypocrisies and arrogant questions.

I'm going to stand. Rise against the internal current that I can't help. Knowing I was responsible.

Made in the USA
Monee, IL
17 August 2025

22383166R00135